Slocum had been prepared for a fight, but Tulley still took him by surprise. Instead of trying to stand, the man kicked out. A heavy boot struck Slocum just under the knee. His left leg buckled painfully under him. As he stumbled, the pistol left its deadly sighting between Tulley's pig eyes. This momentary lapse was all it took for the bounty hunter to surge to his feet.

"I'm gonna rip your head off," Tulley promised. He lumbered forward, murder in his eye . . . .

OTHER BOOKS BY JAKE LOGAN

JAKE LOGAN

THE GRANDVILLE
BANK HEIST

BERKLEY BOOKS, NEW YORK

THE GRANDVILLE BANK HEIST

A Berkley Book / published by arrangement with
the author

PRINTING HISTORY
Berkley edition / October 1991

ISBN: 0-425-12971-3

A BERKLEY BOOK® TM 757,375
Berkley Books are published by The Berkley Publishing Group,
200 Madison Avenue, New York, New York 10016.
The name "BERKLEY" and the "B" logo
are trademarks belonging to Berkley Publishing Corporation.

PRINTED IN THE UNITED STATES OF AMERICA

10 9 8 7 6 5 4 3 2 1

1

John Slocum wiped the gritty dust from his face as he entered the Lone Star Saloon. Every damn saloon in West Texas carried the same name, he thought. If it wasn't the Lone Star, then it was the Longhorn or the Branch Water. But names didn't matter to him right now. He was sore from riding and dog tired. He couldn't remember when he had ever felt so exhausted.

"Wet your whistle, mister?" asked the barkeep. "We got some good Kain-tuck whiskey under the bar."

Slocum laughed without humor. "I don't have enough money for that," he said. It didn't take a genius to know any liquor served in this town had never seen the gentle green hills of Kentucky. He knew he wasn't likely to get more than trade whiskey in this godforsaken place. He couldn't even remember the name of the town on the simple, crudely lettered signpost he'd noticed as he'd ridden in.

"Beer's a nickel," the barkeep said, sizing up Slocum's poke. "And lunch is free. We got pigs' knuckles and pretzels. All the pickles are long gone. Had a hungry crowd in today."

Slocum slapped a half dime down on the counter and

1

indicated that the beer was exactly what he wanted. When it came it was thin and warm, and it tasted like the finest wine he'd ever poured down his gullet. He had ridden from San Angelo and got caught in the worst sandstorm he'd ever seen. Anyone with an ounce of good sense would have holed up and let the storm blow over, but not Slocum.

He had received a strange telegram from an old friend, Emmett Vinson, telling him to ride north and west and he'd be contacted along the way. Vinson had hinted at a huge payoff but had stopped short of describing where this fabulous mother lode was to come from. Slocum had ridden with Vinson for over six months and knew the tall, thin, hatchet-faced man was usually honest with his friends and was someone who could always sniff out the lucrative deal, even if it was a bit on the shady side.

Slocum chuckled to himself as he remembered the times spent riding with Vinson. The man seemed to get an especially big thrill out of any deal that was illegal. He was always looking for the angle, and he sometimes made it pay off big. Too many of Slocum's acquaintances never reached the pot of gold at the end of their rainbow because they were too greedy. Vinson had a streak of avarice in him, but he tempered daring with good sense.

Since it was time to ride on anyway, Slocum decided he had nothing to lose if he played along with Vinson's odd request. He had been riding for over a week and had checked the telegraph offices in three towns, all to no avail. Slocum wasn't even sure if he was heading in the right direction. Vinson hadn't been too specific about where they were going to rendezvous.

"Doesn't it ever rain in Texas?" he asked the barkeep. "There's not so much as a hint of water out in those clouds."

"Clouds? I ain't seen a cloud in well nigh a week," the man answered. He stroked his long handlebar mustache. "We're in the middle of a two-year drought. If this goes on much longer, I'm gonna have to prime myself before I can spit." The barkeep stared out the door into the windy street. "Reckon we could use some rain, but when it comes we're as likely to get it all in an hour's spell. It's either drought or a real frog strangler. No in-between, no sir, not in Texas."

Slocum looked around the saloon and knew this wasn't the place where he could earn a decent wage. The disconsolate men sitting at the tables weren't gambling. That meant there wasn't even enough for penny-ante poker, not that he was rich enough for a high stakes game himself. Slocum touched his vest pocket. He had twenty cents left to his name. Even if this no-name town had a hotel, he wasn't likely to be able to afford a bed and a bath.

"Nope," the bartender said, answering his unspoken question, "ain't jobs around here, either. Most of them fellers are out of work. The ranchers have to cut back on the herds when the water dries up. That means everybody suffers. They don't buy much when they come to town and there's not much to drive north to the Kansas railheads come spring."

"They're all cowhands," Slocum said, pointing toward the knot of men with his beer mug. He knew the look. He could work a herd with the best of them, but there wasn't a one inside the saloon who wouldn't work for just the grub offered. Slocum would want money besides the food. That the men were here and not on the range told him there wasn't any job available.

Maybe he could make it to Denver. The thriving mountain city always had something available. He was beginning to think Vinson had sent him on a wild-goose chase. That wasn't Vinson's style, but maybe something had come up. Slocum had expected to see his old friend pop up from behind every mesquite or creosote bush along the trail.

All he had seen were rattlers dying of thirst.

"You look mighty familiar," the barkeep said suddenly. "You ain't from around here, though."

"Lot of men got my face," Slocum said, suddenly wary. He'd never seen the bartender before. If the man wasn't just talking to hear his own voice, that meant a wanted poster had floated through recently. Maybe Vinson had asked around for him, but Slocum doubted that. Emmett was a cautious man in such matters. He showed incredible daring when it counted, but he knew how dangerous it was to inquire after a man in the company of strangers. There were too many sheriffs looking to collect a reward to augment their paltry salaries.

"Not around these parts," the barkeep said. He stared at Slocum as if he could force the memory to return. Slocum saw the effort fail and relaxed a mite. If he couldn't find a poker game or get a job here, it was time to move on. He didn't like it when people tried to remember who he was.

"You got a telegraph station here? I saw lines running into town, but the damned thing's usually out in most towns."

"We got one. Last I saw of old Red—he's the telegrapher—he was snoring to beat the band. No traffic coming through. That's the way he talks, as if listening to them little clicks and clacks on his key count as traffic."

Slocum finished the beer, gnawed on a pig's knuckle and passed on the pretzel. It was stale and had too much salt on it. The only reason the barkeep kept it handy was to make the offer and maybe find some fool who'd eat it and need another beer to slake the thirst it would provoke. Slocum considered another beer, but time was beginning to press in on him now.

"Down the street, over by the sheriff's office," the barkeep said. "Can't miss it. Huge sign outside."

"Thanks," Slocum said. "I reckon I'll be back in a spell for another beer."

"I'll keep it cold for you," the barkeep lied. He went back to polishing glasses with a dirty rag, his one brief diversion gone. The other men in the saloon weren't talkative sorts.

Slocum eyed the sheriff's office with some disdain. Whoever let himself take a job like sheriff in this one-horse town wasn't too good at much of anything. But the barkeep saying he thought he recognized him kept Slocum cautious. He never knew when a new wanted poster was going to make the rounds. He had ridden a straight trail recently, but a year back he had gotten tangled up with a Texas Ranger.

Texas Rangers had long memories, and the printing press down in Austin kept cranking out warrants day and night, or so it seemed to Slocum.

He skirted the sheriff's office and went to the telegraph office. Sure as the drought had seared the grama grass out on the range, the barkeep was right. The telegrapher sat at his desk, arms folded and his head resting on them. He snored so loudly he drowned out the chatter of the telegraph key.

"You open for business?" Slocum asked.

"Eh, what's that?" The telegrapher jerked upright. A shock of wild red hair sneaked out from under his visor.

"Been trying to reach a friend, but he's moving too fast for me. Reckon he's been trying to reach me, too. He knew I was riding this way." Slocum wished to hell he could remember the name of the town.

"Who be you?" Red asked, rubbing his eyes. He fumbled around and found a pair of reading glasses. He balanced them on the tip of his nose as he peered at Slocum.

"Name's Slocum."

"Hasn't been much traffic lately, but there was one message that was right strange. Came as a down-the-wire."

"What's that?" Slocum asked.

"A telegram that's sent to every station on the line. Usually a 'gram just goes to one place. The other folks along the wire ignore it and wait for their own traffic, but a down-the-wire is sent to every town. Yep, here it is. Slocum, you said?" Red peered at him again, as if he might be lying.

"That's my name."

"Got this here down-the-wire telegram for you, then. From somebody what only signed it with his initials."

"If the initials are E. V., then I reckon my friend's found me."

"Those are the initials," the telegrapher said, holding up the thin sheet of yellow paper. "The flimsy's yours for the price of ten cents."

"But—" Slocum cut off his protest. He'd thought the telegram would have been paid for. He fished in his pocket and pulled out a dime and handed it to Red. The man took it, peered at it skeptically, then slipped it into his vest pocket. He handed the telegram to Slocum.

Slocum spread it out on the counter and read the few words. He crumpled the sheet in disgust. Vinson was playing some strange game with him, and he didn't know what it was. And since it had just cost him ten of the fifteen cents he had left, Slocum wasn't too inclined to play along.

"Grandville's north of here about fifty miles," Red said. The telegrapher got a frightened look when Slocum turned on him. Cold green eyes bored into the man's soul. "I had to read it. Hell, man, I copied it off the wire. I had to know what was in it."

"Thanks," Slocum said, not meaning it. He started to leave when Red called out, "Say, Mr. Slocum, ain't I seen you around here before? You surely do look familiar."

Slocum turned in the doorway and studied the telegrapher. He had never seen Red before, either. First the barkeep and now the town's telegrapher. What was going on?

"There been someone through here looking for me? Is that it?" he demanded. The telegrapher turned pale and stepped back, his hand reaching for a desk drawer. Slocum knew that was where the telegraph company's six-shooter must be kept.

He slid the Colt Navy from his cross-draw holster in a smooth action faster than Red could follow.

"I asked a question. Who's been looking for me? Describe him."

"He—he's got a wanted poster. Your picture's on it. Don't know his name. Big, ugly brute. Stands an inch taller'n you and must weigh half again as much. And he smells."

This startled Slocum. In the middle of a two-year-long drought, nobody took baths. For the man's body odor to be remembered, it must be very bad.

"You have a name to go with the description?"

"No sir, Mr. Slocum, I surely don't. He came through a week or more back asking about you."

Slocum dropped his six-shooter back into the soft leather holster and spun. He waited to hear the telltale squeaking of the desk drawer if Red decided to get lucky. There was only the man's harsh breathing. Slocum stepped into the dusty street and knew he had to move on.

"Damn you, Emmett Vinson, what the hell do you want from me?" Slocum muttered to himself. Grandville was a good two days' ride to the north. Maybe more, if the infernal wind didn't let up. And now he had a man on his trail. From the description the telegrapher gave, it wasn't a Texas Ranger. For this small favor Slocum was grateful. Rangers never stopped hunting for their prey.

But a bounty hunter might be as bad. Slocum tried to put a name or a face to the description and couldn't, but he knew the bounty hunter had picked up his trail recently. He'd spent almost a month in San Angelo not doing much of anything. That had to be where someone had recognized him or where the bounty hunter had finally caught up with him. Before

San Angelo, Slocum had cut a wide swath through the Piney Woods of East Texas. He had run afoul of a regulator group there, but it wasn't anything too serious. Not as serious as killing a judge.

Slocum walked toward the saloon where his horse was still tethered. It was time to ride on, maybe to Grandville, maybe to Denver, but it was time to be out of this nameless hamlet. Judge killing was serious business, even if the crime was years old and hundreds of miles away.

After the war, he had returned to the family farm in Calhoun, Georgia, thinking to settle down as a farmer. A carpetbagger judge had taken a shine to the Slocum farm, thinking it would make a fine horse ranch. No taxes had been paid during the war, the judge said. He and a hired gunman had ridden from town to take the farm away from Slocum.

Slocum had ridden out just before sundown, and there were two fresh graves out by the springhouse. He was only a crooked damned Yankee judge, but the law didn't care about such niceties. An officer of the court was dead by John Slocum's hand, and that was good enough to begin a long string of warrants placed for his arrest.

"Which warrant has this bounty hunter found?" Slocum wondered aloud as he put his foot into the stirrup to mount.

"Turn around and you're buzzard bait," came a cold voice. "I got a double-barreled shotgun aimed at your back."

2

Slocum's mind raced. He was in an awkward position to be able to turn and draw. If the man behind him—and he figured it was the bounty hunter—was telling the truth about the shotgun, he'd be cut into hamburger before he got his pistol halfway out of its holster.

There wasn't any other option open to him but to surrender. And it galled him to be caught this easily, especially after he had been thinking about the man chasing him.

"You touch that fancy-ass black-handled pistol of yours and you're dead," the man said in an agitated voice. "Now get that foot of yours on out of the stirrup and turn around. I want to see you reaching for sky as you do."

Slocum obeyed. He faced a man with a huge leveled shotgun and the most truculent look on his face of any man he'd ever encountered. The bounty hunter stood half a head taller and three times as wide. Slocum looked for a hint that some of the bulk was fat. He didn't find it. The man was a mountain of solid muscle and he looked mean.

"You John Slocum?"

"You got me confused with somebody else, mister," Slocum said.

"My name's Tulley. I reckon you got a right to know the man what's takin' you in to have your neck stretched."

"What's going on here? You with the shotgun. Put it down this instant."

A bandy-legged man wearing a battered tin sheriff's star bustled up. This was all the diversion Slocum needed. He knew he couldn't get to his six-shooter fast enough to matter. He took a single step forward and kicked for all he was worth. The roar of the shotgun deafened Slocum. That he heard the thunder from the long-barreled weapon told Slocum he was still alive. He stepped inside the bounty hunter's flailing arms and drove his rock-hard fist squarely into Tulley's face. There was a liquid squish followed by an ear-splitting roar of pain.

"You son of a bitch! You busted my goddamn nose!"

Slocum didn't stop to see what damage he had done. Blood covered his hand. He cocked back and let fly another punch straight to Tulley's midriff. This was a mistake. Slocum felt the shock all the way up to his shoulder. Hitting the man's belly was like trying to punch through rock with his bare hands.

"Stop it. What's going on? I do say, stop this altercation instantly!"

Slocum blinked as he turned and saw the prissy sheriff out of the corner of his eye.

"This man's wanted by the law over in Tyler," Tulley grunted out. He kept one hand over his gushing nose. "I got a right. I got the arrest warrant and all. It's legal."

While the bounty hunter argued with the sheriff over legal niceties, Slocum was swinging again. This time he didn't aim for the slab-like belly. He swung his clenched fist against the bounty hunter's left temple. The blow staggered the mountain of a man. Tulley wobbled, then fell to his knees, stunned.

The mincing sheriff had no chance to pull his six-shooter

and stop Slocum. The blow had rocked Slocum back, but he recovered swiftly. He turned, gauged the distance to the lawman, and then let loose another kick. He caught the sheriff in the crotch.

The sheriff gulped, bent double, and then turned green as he sank to the ground. Slocum knew he wasn't making any friends in this town. That meant it was time to ride on out. He looked over at Tulley and wondered if he should do anything more to the man—like put a bullet between his piglike eyes.

Only trouble rode with him when he left an enemy behind alive. In the short time it took Slocum to consider killing Tulley, a crowd began to form. It wasn't the right place to finish off the bounty hunter. Slocum doubted if Tulley was the kind to give up easily, but he might have second thoughts about coming after this prey.

Slocum kicked out again. The toe of his boot caught the bounty hunter under the chin and snapped his head back with a loud pop. Before he hit the ground, Slocum was rummaging through the man's pockets. He found a thick wallet tucked just inside the uncured hide shirt he wore. The stench rising from both jacket and man was overpowering. Slocum knew this had to be the man who the telegrapher had described.

Pulling out a sheaf of papers, Slocum riffled through them. He found two wanted posters with his likeness and an arrest warrant issued by the East Texas Regulators Society for his arrest. Slocum hadn't even realized they wanted him for anything, much less a crime as picayune as cattle rustling. East Texas was ablaze with a war between rival vigilante groups, all vying for control. Slocum was unfortunate enough to have run afoul of the wrong group.

He stuffed the warrant and the two posters into his shirt, then jumped into his saddle. The tired roan he had bought in San Angelo shied. He kept a firm grip on the reins.

"Hey, you, wait," called someone from near the general store. Another man on the boardwalk was fumbling to get out his hogleg. It was time to be away from this sleepy, dusty town. Slocum put his spurs into the horse's flanks. The strawberry roan tried to rear, then exploded into a full gallop.

Slocum let the horse run itself out. He couldn't keep up the gallop for more than a mile without the horse dying under him. That was the last thing Slocum wanted right now. He left the outskirts of the town, then eased up on the spurring. Within a dozen yards the roan began to slow. Inside fifty yards it was down to a brisk walk, which was just fine with Slocum. It gave the horse a chance to regain its breath and Slocum a chance to think.

"What a hellhole," he muttered, looking back over his shoulder at the town. For a place that had absolutely nothing to offer, Slocum had come damned close to getting himself killed. And for what? He fished out the arrest warrant and began tearing it into small pieces. The two wanted posters were from Kansas, one for bank robbery and the other for rustling. To Slocum they didn't amount to a hill of beans. The reward on each was only one hundred dollars.

Even with the regulators' warrant, Tulley couldn't have been looking at more than three hundred dollars for bringing Slocum to justice. Slocum shook his head. Three hundred wasn't much for the misery the bounty hunter would go through trying to collect it.

He slowed his pace even more as he tore the wanted posters into thin strips and let the hot West Texas wind carry them off. Slocum considered turning to the north and west and going to El Paso. From there he could ride up through Santa Fe and into Colorado. Denver was looking more and more attractive. This part of Texas had grown too hot for him to stand much longer, unless he wanted to plug Tulley and maybe the town's sheriff.

At the notion of the sheriff forming a posse and coming after him, Slocum laughed. The man was too timid to be a real lawman. Even in this hot country he'd have cold feet—and that suited Slocum just fine.

He turned more northerly, thinking about the telegram he'd got from Vinson. Emmett was a good man and he might be on to something special. With only a nickel in his pocket, Slocum knew he couldn't run too far. Rustling a few head in this country would be a boon to the rancher, but there might not be a ready buyer this side of the border. Running even a few head south of the border to sell them for ten dollars each wasn't his idea of making money.

"What have you come up with, Emmett you old son of a gun?" The more he considered his options, the more Slocum liked the idea of teaming up with Emmett Vinson again. The days they had ridden together had been good ones, rich ones filled with bulging mailbags loaded with money and strongboxes brimming with gold dust. Nobody had gotten rich, but they'd done well enough.

What more could a man ask?

Slocum started looking for a stock pond to water his mount. For that matter, he was feeling the insidious grit from the trail working its way back into his own mouth. The beer had done little to cut his savage thirst.

He walked the roan up a rise and looked around, wondering if the stock tanks would be guarded. In such a severe drought, they might be, and he wasn't likely to buy any water with just a nickel in his pocket. Slocum slowly scanned the horizon. Thick brown dust clouds cloaked much of it, but he finally saw a circular tank a mile off. Urging his horse toward it proved easy. The animal's nostrils flared as it scented water and it kept trying to gallop. Slocum had to work to hold it back.

As he rode up, he saw that there wasn't much water in

the stock pond. Hardly enough stood to cause mud in the bottom, but it was more than he was likely to get elsewhere. Slocum let the roan drink its fill; he didn't worry about it bloating. If it drank all the water, it wouldn't do more than get its tongue wet.

Slocum rummaged through his saddlebags and found an old shirt. The threadbare cloth was exactly what he needed now. He sat on a rock next to the muddy pond bottom and held his canteen between his knees. Slopping mud into his shirt, he let the water slowly ooze through and drip into the canteen. It was a laborious process but the result would keep him alive for the two days it took to reach Grandville and Emmett Vinson's new scheme.

Working methodically, Slocum filled his canteen and wondered if he had anything else that would hold water, even for a few hours. This was likely to be all the water he would see for some time.

The strawberry roan lifted its nose and let out a loud whinny. This brought Slocum around, his hand flying to the ebony handle of his six-shooter.

"Damnation," he cursed under his breath. A new dust cloud was added to the naturally occurring one kicked up by the wind. A rider or maybe two approached from the far side of the stock pond. Whoever it was meant trouble for John Slocum.

Being arrested on an old wanted poster or shot for stealing water during a drought seemed the only two possibilities. Neither pleased him. Slocum mounted and rode around the stock pond, putting the high mound of earth between him and the approaching riders. They came from the east rather than from the south. He hoped this meant that they weren't from the town.

"There he is, Sheriff!" came the bellowing cry that

drowned out even the insistent hot wind. "I'll get that son of a bitch!"

Slocum swung around and saw that Tulley had reached the earthen rim of the stock tank and was able to see him. Slocum got off a quick shot that spooked his horse but did nothing to stop the bounty hunter's headlong charge down the side of the tank.

Seeing that it was ridiculous to make a stand here, Slocum got his horse into a run that wouldn't tire it too soon. A wind-cut arroyo some distance away looked like the best place for him to make a stand—if he could reach it before Tulley got to him.

As he rode, Slocum considered his options. Cutting down the bounty hunter looked to be the best of the lot. He hated having to look over his shoulder as he rode. If the sheriff got the bee into his bonnet that Slocum was a desperado worthy of forming a posse, then Slocum would never escape. The promise of even a dollar a day for posse duty would look like manna from heaven to the unemployed cowboys. Hell, for that much money they'd even stretch his neck as part of the bargain.

Slocum had to laugh at that thought. There weren't even cottonwood trees out here tall enough for a man to properly hang. They'd have to build a gallows if they wanted to hang him!

He hit the ground running when he saw the jagged edge of the arroyo. His horse kept running a few more yards and then came to a halt. Slocum had pulled his Winchester from its saddle sheath and was levering a round into the chamber when he saw the behemoth bounty hunter coming out of the dust cloud.

Slocum had to take a deep, calming breath to remind himself that Tulley was only human. He might look like a berserk

Indian spirit as he rode hell-bent for leather, but he would die just like any other man taking a bullet in his head.

Sighting carefully, Slocum squeezed the trigger, and the rifle bucked in his grip. He knew the instant he fired that the shot had gone wide. Tulley didn't slow his breakneck attack. He came on, whooping and hollering like a Comanche brave. Slocum got off a second shot that tore away part of Tulley's left sleeve. He kept riding. Another man would have been spooked by the attack.

Slocum had gone through the war as a sniper and had learned patience. He levered a third round into the chamber and waited. The range had been too great for such a rapidly moving target. When Tulley was less than twenty yards away, Slocum fired again.

This round took the bounty hunter out of his saddle. He flew backward off his horse and landed hard on the ground. Slocum doubted the slug had taken the man's life. It didn't have a "killing feel" to it, but the round had stopped the attack. For the moment, that was good enough.

Slocum stood and peered over the arroyo's bank for some glimpse of the sheriff. Where the lawman had gotten off to, he couldn't say. From everything he had seen of him in town, it wouldn't surprise Slocum if the sheriff had hightailed it back to his friends.

He fetched his horse and mounted, wondering if he ought to check Tulley to be sure the bounty hunter was dead. The slug he had put into the man hadn't killed him outright. Still, a round festering in a man's gut would do the same chore, if a mite slower. Slocum wasn't the kind to let any man linger if he could put him out of his misery.

Still, the sheriff was around somewhere. That bothered him.

"Hell," Slocum said to himself. "I wouldn't let a horse with a broken leg suffer. No reason a bounty hunter deserves less." He urged his roan up the steep bank of the arroyo and across the dusty stretch to where the bounty hunter ought to have been.

Slocum blinked as dust filled his eyes. He couldn't believe Tulley had heaved himself up and run off, but he must have. There wasn't a trace of the man anywhere. Slocum back-tracked a ways, got to the stock tank, and circled it, hunting for any trace of either the sheriff or the bounty hunter. He found nothing to show that either man had ever existed.

"If that don't beat all," Slocum said, patting his horse on the neck. The sheriff might have turned tail and run back to town where he'd be safe, but what about Tulley?

Slocum didn't like loose ends—and the bounty hunter was a big one.

3

The next day's ride found Slocum tired, dirty, and almost delirious from acute thirst. The lingering drought had sucked every possible drop of water from the Texas land. He found cattle dead along the road, their carcasses looking like tanned leather. There hadn't even been enough interest from buzzards to come down and peck away at them because of their desiccation. Only the ever-present ants found a decent meal in the sun- and wind-dried bodies.

Slocum knew it wouldn't take much more wind and burning sun before he found himself added to the menagerie of roadside dead. He rolled a small pebble around in his mouth to keep what little moisture he could flowing over his tongue. The smooth rock had long since started to taste bitterly metallic, a sure sign he'd need water soon or pass out from thirst.

In spite of his dryness, Slocum occasionally turned and backtracked to be sure neither the sheriff nor the bounty hunter were on his trail. He was getting antsy about them. Tulley hadn't simply blown away like a dead leaf with the dust cloud. The man had crawled off, and Slocum had missed him. But he wasn't dead. Slocum knew that deep down in his gut. And he also knew he hadn't seen the last of the persistent bounty hunter. No man gets humiliated in public and then shot down like a mad dog and simply forgets about it. He had a big score to settle with Slocum, and the huge bounty hunter looked like the kind who carried grudges a long, long time. It might be better to simply up and die of thirst than to let Tulley capture him again. Getting back to a town with a judge for trial would be an arduous trek that would make the road to Grandville look like a spring picnic.

As to the banty rooster sheriff, he had been humiliated, too. Slocum wondered if it mattered to the man, though. He didn't seem the sort to have much of a standing, even in the one-horse Texas town that had pinned the tin star on his chest.

Slocum found himself thinking of the difference between the two men. The sheriff was the kind who would sneak up behind him and fire a single round into the back of his head. Tulley lacked any subtlety, but the man had gumption, and he didn't look to be the kind to ever back down from a fight. If anything, he'd relish it.

"A backshooter and a bounty hunter," muttered Slocum. He pulled his dirty bandanna up around his nose to keep more of the invasive dust from his nostrils. It didn't work. The dust slipped into every crevice of his body and gritted like sandpaper. He needed more than a bath; he needed complete irrigation to feel normal.

"You better have a damned good plan, Emmett Vinson," he said to the wind. "And if you're not in Grandville, I'll track you down to the corners of the earth to make you pay for this." Slocum bowed his head as a new gust drove flesh-cutting grit into his face.

He rode like this for so long he almost missed the steel rim in the middle of the road. His roan sidestepped it, prancing and snorting. Slocum blinked and looked down to see what had attracted the attention of his horse. The steel rim had once belonged to a wagon. If it had come off, that meant the wheel had followed soon after. There wasn't any way in hell a bare wooden wheel was going to roll over this rocky road for very long without falling apart.

Slocum hadn't gone a quarter mile when his guess was confirmed. A small wagon rested on its side, its right back wheel broken to splinters. The pitiful belongings in the wagon bed had been scattered across the prairie. The wind had done the rest, sending the contents into ground-clinging mesquite bushes.

Slocum smiled when he saw the type of clothing dangling in tatters from the thorny trees. A woman of some wealth and breeding had lost her unmentionables. But of the woman Slocum couldn't find a trace. He doubted she would have gone far in the windstorm. No one could have done so without getting turned around.

He slid from his horse and examined the wagon. The axle had broken when the wheel finally split. In the wind the driver probably hadn't noticed the steel rim coming loose. The rocky road would have made it doubly difficult to feel that anything was wrong with the rig. But the single horse that had been pulling the wagon was gone.

Examining the harness, Slocum couldn't tell if the horse had pulled free when the wagon overturned or if the driver had cut the horse loose. If so, that might explain the disappearance of the wagon's driver, who might have mounted the horse and tried to ride into Grandville.

Even over the whistle of the wind, Slocum heard the distinctive sound of a six-shooter being cocked. He kept up the pretense of checking the wagon, moving so that he could get to his Colt.

"Don't," came the somewhat shrill voice. "I'll put a bullet in the back of your head if you try turning."

That was a hard shot, even for a marksman. Slocum decided to chance it. He started turning, his hand sliding toward his pistol.

The bullet ripped a piece of wood from the wagon barely an inch from his nose.

"I hit what I aim at."

"Can you do it again?" Slocum asked, startled by the nearness of the slug and the gunman's calm reply.

The second bullet made him jump back. The lead had gouged out a second hole in the side of the wagon not an inch from the first. Slocum knew when to give up. He slowly raised his hands in defeat.

"Down on your knees. I don't want you boltin' like an unbroke filly." The words were more distinct now. A woman had the drop on him, probably the same one who had lost her undies in the wind.

"Don't reckon I want to die like that. Either shoot me in the heart or not at all, but I won't die on my knees."

Slocum turned slowly, his hands still above his head. For a moment he and the woman simply stared at each other. She was tall and willowy. He saw every contour of her body as the wind held her thin dress against her. A long black mane of hair whipped in the wind and the bluest of blue eyes stared at him in disbelief. The Colt .44 she held in her right hand never wavered. She knew how to use the thumb-buster and showed every inclination of being able to make good on her promise to plug him if he looked at her cross-eyed.

"Haven't seen you in a while, Marla," Slocum said.

"Haven't seen you in a while either, John," she answered.

"We didn't leave on the best of terms, but there's no reason for you to drill me, is there?"

"Sorry," she said, lowering the heavy six-shooter. "This wind has got me spooked something fierce. And lower your hands. You look like a damn fool standing there like that."

"It wasn't to my liking, but I surely do appreciate your expert marksmanship. When you fired that second round I ought to have known it was you. You're just about the only woman I ever saw who could outshoot me."

"Pshaw," she said, averting her eyes modestly. "That's not true, but it's nice of you to say it. And we didn't part on such bad terms. About all I remember is that there wasn't a properly said good-bye."

"There wasn't much time for that," Slocum allowed. He tried to figure what kind of fate it was that he'd met up with Emmett Vinson's sister again. Marla Vinson was one fine looking woman, and she had qualities Slocum truly admired. The last time he had seen her was well nigh three years back, a month after he and Emmett had ridden different trails.

"Kansas City," she said. "That's where it was."

"Since you're here, I assume the posse never caught you," Slocum said. He had managed to get to the river after they were separated by the posse and had hitched a ride downriver to New Orleans. It had bothered him leaving the woman behind to fend for herself, but if anyone could have eluded the posse, it was Marla Vinson.

"I doubled back on them, then managed to get some new clothing and just faded into the Kansas City crowds. It took a spell, but they weren't looking for a washerwoman. They never came close to finding me, but you were gone."

"You were dressed as a man then," Slocum remembered. "A crime, if ever there was one. You ought to dress just about like you are now." He appreciated the way the wind held her dress against her trim body. He saw every curve and crevice as she moved to come closer to him. Nipples stood out in bold relief as the thin fabric strained hard and whipped in the hot wind.

"What are you staring at, John?"

"I was envying the wind," he said. He slid his arm around her waist and drew her near. Marla looked up, her eyes shining. Then they closed and her lips parted slightly. Slocum didn't need any more invitation to give her a kiss. It wasn't as satisfying as he'd thought. The damnable dust got everywhere, including in both their mouths.

They separated, sputtering and laughing.

"We've got to get out of this wind," she said. "I've been looking for water for the past two days and haven't had much luck."

"I've got a little left in my canteen. You're welcome to it." Slocum had to speak through cracked lips, but the offer was sincere. His only regret was that he didn't have more to give her.

"I'm fine. It's my horse," she said. "When the wagon tipped over, it tore free of its harness and bolted. I don't have the foggiest idea where it got off to."

"In this wind, it could be anywhere. Do you know how far we are from Grandville?"

She looked at him and said, "Emmett got in touch with you, didn't he? You're going to Grandville because he asked."

"Aren't you going there for the same reason?"

"Yes. But Emmett didn't tell me you were in on the robbery. I'd've been there a month ago if he'd so much as hinted at that. You know how I feel about you, John. And if you don't, you're a fool."

"A fool?" Slocum asked.

"No, not a fool. You might be many things but never a fool," she said. She threw her arms around him and hugged him close. "We're about ten miles outside town, but the windstorm's getting worse. If we have to make it on one horse, it might be better to hole up until the storm's blowed itself out."

Slocum saw that this was the prudent thing to do, but his thirst raged on unabated.

"I'm a bit lightheaded from lack of water. My horse isn't in any better shape," he told her. "We might as well push on and—"

"You haven't had any water and you're offering me some of your canteen. I do declare, John Slocum. And I thought Southern gentlemen were a thing of the past."

"What do you mean?"

"Hunker on down here and try this." Marla pulled a long hose from under the wagon. She sucked on it for a few seconds then held it up for him. Precious water bubbled from the end of the tube. Like a mountain lion spotting a meal, Slocum pounced on the water. He greedily guzzled it until the natural moisture returned to his mouth. Sticking his thumb in the tube, he held it out to her.

"No, that's all right. I've been drinking it for some time. Why do you think I brought a wagon? I can ride with the best of 'em, John. I needed it to ship water. I had damned near fifty gallons in the back when I left Dallas last week."

"Fifty gallons," he marveled. "Do you have enough left to let my horse have a sip or two?"

"Not enough for a horse," she said. "I've been looking for water to fill my empty kegs, but there hasn't been any. We've got to get under cover or the dust will strip the flesh from our bones. I do declare, I've never seen such wind in all my days."

They went to the lee side of the overturned wagon. Slocum then saw the wood kegs Marla had carried. Several had broken open when the wagon wheel broke, but one was intact. It was enough to give to his roan and still enjoy a feast of the wonderfully wet liquid himself.

"We can pull this tarpaulin over and pin it to the ground," she said. Marla tugged at the flapping canvas and showed

Slocum what she intended. The rude lean-to would be formed using the wagon bed as one side. The canvas flapped loudly but was held securely enough when Slocum finished with it. Crawling under it gave them shelter from the omnipresent dust and wind.

"My horse," he said.

"Let him stand in the lee out of the direct blast of the wind," she said. "Any shelter's better than none in this wind, and it doesn't look as if he's had any of late."

Slocum saw that the strawberry roan was as well taken care of as could be out on the range. He silently promised the valiant animal real grain when they got to Grandville. It deserved that and all the water it could drink for enduring such hardship.

"This is better," Marla said, settling down on her bedroll. "I thought I'd have to walk into Grandville. That's no way to make a grand entrance into a grand city."

"If it's like the other towns I've seen out here, it's misnamed," Slocum said.

"Not so misnamed," Marla said, her fingers stroking his wind-burned cheek. "You know what Emmett's planned."

"No, I don't," Slocum said.

Marla's eyes widened. "That's a surprise. He trusts you implicitly. I reckon I'll have to tell you."

"Let's discuss it later," Slocum said, leaning back. He pulled the woman down to him. She kissed him passionately, and he returned in kind. The wind howled above them but they drifted away to a world occupied only by the pair of them.

Slocum wasn't sure how it happened, but he found his finger gliding over bare flesh, warm and willing female flesh. Marla gasped when his hand ventured along her ribs and worked even lower. He touched the spot between her legs and she arched her back and moaned softly.

"Feels like I've struck water," he said. "Sure is getting moist down there."

"Drink all you want, John," she whispered hotly as she began nibbling at his ear.

Slocum discovered a second miracle. He was not quite certain how it happened, but Marla skinned him out of his dirty clothing. His bare skin glided across hers as they rolled over and over, kissing, teasing, nibbling and exciting one another.

"There, John, feel me there." She pulled his hand back to the firm inner surface of her thigh, then raised it back to where the dampness welled. His fingers wiggled to and fro and caused her to gasp. Marla rolled over and this time Slocum found himself atop the woman, between her wantonly spread legs.

"Do it, John. I want it. You want it, too. I can tell." She gripped his rigid length. There was no mistaking either of their desires.

He moved easily, positioning himself. The end of his fleshy pillar brushed across her nether lips. She shivered deliciously and began scratching at his back with her fingernails. The motion drove him wild with need. His hips levered forward, and he sank balls deep in her clutching interior. They both gasped at the sudden intimate intrusion.

For a long minute, Slocum simply hung suspended, reveling in the sensations blasting through his body. The way his balls tightened told him he'd have to do more soon or neither of them would be truly satisfied. He pulled back slowly, tormenting her with his length, making her sob with need.

Then he came rushing back in so fast he lifted the fleshy globes of her buttocks off the bedroll. Her long legs circled his waist and tried to pull him in even deeper.

"Don't stop now," she whispered huskily. "I need it, I need you so much, John!"

He gave her what they both needed. He began stroking with the age-old motion of a man loving a woman. The wind howled and the dust blew and Slocum and Marla's pulses raced.

The faster he moved, the more his passions built. He became one with the wild elements just a few feet away. He soared and blazed inside, his loins afire. Marla began raking at his back, spurring him on with her silent pleas for more, ever more.

He exploded within her like a stick of dynamite going off. Seconds later, she arched her back and ground her crotch down hard into his, her pleasure matching his. Only after they had both peaked did they relax and lie side by side on the bedroll.

Slocum's arm circled the woman's shoulders as she moved closer. Her head rested on his bare chest. She said something he missed in the howl of the wind and then slipped into a contented sleep. Slocum held her tight and just stared up at the flapping canvas above them. It had been too long.

Sleep came along with speculations on Marla and her brother Emmett and what lay ahead in Grandville.

4

"Thank heavens the dust has let up," Marla Vinson said. She shook her head and a tiny shower of dust billowed like a miniature sandstorm in the morning sun. Slocum realized he needed a bath, too. The thought came to him that taking a bath with the lovely dark-haired woman would be just about the next best thing to paradise.

"I'm glad there was a keg of water unbroken," he said. He had poked open the keg right after sunrise and let his roan drink its fill. He and Marla had finished it off and then he had transferred what was left in a second to his canteen. Even with the cessation of the wind and a settling of the dust, it was hot traveling the road to Grandville.

"It certainly seems to have saved your life," Marla said. "I'm surprised at you, John. You planned better in the old days. You haven't changed, have you?"

"Did I seem different last night?" Slocum asked. Marla inched closer, her arms around his waist. She rode behind him on the horse just as naturally as if she had been there forever.

"Not in any important way," she admitted. "Still, you have

to admit it's a damfool thing to go riding out of a town without more water than what you were carrying."

He hadn't told her about his run-in with the bounty hunter or the sheriff. Slocum started to and then stopped. There wasn't any reason to bother her with what might be a solved problem. The bounty hunter was in worse shape than he was and had even less water. Tulley was probably dead out on the prairie somewhere, his body just waiting for carrion eaters to dine.

"I left the last town in a bit of a hurry," he said.

"The one where you got Emmett's telegram?"

"Don't even remember the town's name," Slocum said. "Fact is, I don't reckon I ever knew it. The telegrapher said Emmett had sent the message to every station along the line."

Marla nodded, knowing her brother's habits. "I got several messages on my way from Dallas," she said. "He did the same thing. And I had to pay for the telegrams!"

Slocum had to laugh at that. Vinson wasn't treating his sister any better than he was an old friend. That made Slocum feel a tad better about what lay ahead. Vinson was working hard at sizing up the robbery and didn't have time for petty things like paying for the telegrams he was sending.

At least, that's what Slocum hoped.

"No, John," she said, answering his unspoken question. "I don't know all the details of what Emmett's planning, but he was never one to go after penny-ante payoffs."

"No," Slocum agreed, "Emmett always tried for the big robbery. One or two of them even worked like he promised. Seems to me he has a tendency to outfox himself by planning too much."

"You can never plan too much," Marla said, as if reciting a lesson learned a long time back. "He's real cautious, but not when it matters. You know him."

"I do know Emmett Vinson," Slocum said, but his

thoughts were turning more to the sister. He enjoyed riding with the woman's arms wrapped around his waist. The day was hot and he was sweating like a pig, but her warm nearness still appealed to him. Slocum hadn't realized how much he had missed her until he had seen her pointing that six-shooter at him back at the wagon.

He daydreamed about how it might have been if they hadn't been separated back in Kansas. He had taken a leisurely trip down the Mississippi River and had spent the entire trip thinking about Marla. New Orleans had gone a long way toward erasing her from his mind, but he knew now that the intervening years hadn't completely wiped out the pleasant memories.

And last night's lovemaking rekindled what had been smoldering for all those years.

"So I don't know much more than you, but Emmett's always clever in these things," Slocum heard the woman saying. He had drifted along and hadn't been paying attention. He didn't think it mattered too much. The day was too hot for anyone to think straight.

"There's the edge of town," he said. Buildings rising from the prairie told him that Grandville wasn't far off. "Think they have a decent water supply?"

"I hope so," Marla said earnestly. "There's nothing I need more than a long, hot bath." She tightened her grip around his waist. Slocum knew she was thinking along the same lines he had been earlier. Sharing the bath would save on precious water.

"I need to talk this over with Emmett before I can make a decision," Slocum said.

"But Emmett always—"

"I always want to hear the details before putting my head in a noose. You said it yourself. Emmett comes up with some pretty wild-ass schemes. If this is another one of them, I'm moving on."

"Why so cautious all of a sudden, John?"

He still hadn't told her about the bounty hunter on his trail. All day he had ridden along, looking back occasionally. Marla had thought it was to get a glimpse of her. Slocum had to admit that had been part of his reason. The other was to see if Tulley was hot on his trail. He felt the bounty hunter's presence, even if he hadn't seen him in three days. Slocum wasn't much for killing a man in cold blood, but he wished now he had taken the time to track Tulley down and put a bullet between his piglike eyes.

There's nothing quite as savage as a wounded javelina—and Tulley looked like the worst kind of pig to injure.

"It doesn't pay to stay in one place for too long," he said without giving her a reason. He didn't want to spook her, though he wasn't sure exactly what it might take to spook Marla Vinson. She had courage most men would envy.

"Emmett will make you see the light," she said. "I don't know exactly what he's up to, but it must be good for him to call both of us to Grandville."

Slocum kept riding until he found the town's main street. It was only slightly wider than the side streets. Grandville, Texas, looked no different from a hundred other places he had seen. It might have been dustier, but Slocum wouldn't have even gone that far. He didn't see a railroad station. However they got away after the wonderful robbery Vinson was planning, it would have to be on horseback. That ruled out a gold robbery.

"No gold in this place," Slocum muttered.

"Not gold, maybe," she said, "but there's money here. Take a look down that street."

"That's more like it." Slocum wheeled his roan down the street lined with gaming houses. He counted fourteen before he gave up. This place was wide open. Where there was that kind of gambling activity, there were whores and saloons making obscene amounts of money. Grandville must draw cowboys from all over the panhandle to keep this many houses of ill repute in business.

"I wonder where all the people come from?" Marla asked. "There's got to be something for them to do besides ranching."

"Reckon we'll find out after a spell," Slocum said. "Right now, let's get you settled in a boardinghouse where you can get that bath."

"And a decent meal. I do declare, it's been a month of Sundays since I ate anything that didn't have maggots or dust in it," Marla said.

Slocum rode for the outskirts of town, knowing this was where the more reasonable places would be found. He had a single nickel riding in his pocket. If Marla was to stay anywhere it would have to be on her own money.

"There's a good-looking place," he said, finding a two-story frame house with a white picket fence around it. A Boarders Taken sign was stuck in the front window.

"What about you, John? Aren't you coming in, too? We can always say we're married—unless that bothers you."

"It'd keep the folks from asking too many questions," Slocum allowed, "but the fact is, I don't have two coins to rub together, much less the greenbacks it'd take to stay here. I'll sleep in a stable, if I can find one that'll take my horse without being paid up front."

"I've got a little," Marla said. "You should have said something. You men are always so bullheaded and proud. Here. Take this." She fumbled in her blouse and pulled out a thin roll of greenbacks. Peeling off ten dollars she forced it on Slocum.

"This makes hunting for your brother a sight easier,"

Slocum said. "Emmett's probably in a saloon somewhere keeping his throat wet until we show up."

Marla Vinson dropped to the ground and began unfastening her gear. She looked up at him, her blue eyes sparkling. "When you come back, we'll be registered under Mr. and Mrs. Johnson."

"Why use a summer name?" Slocum asked.

"From the way you kept lookin' back over your shoulder on the road, someone's breathin' heavy down your neck. A bounty hunter, I'd say. Or a sheriff, though they don't stray far. And if you've run afoul of a Ranger, it might be best if you'd just up and tell Emmett so's he can find someone else."

Slocum saw that it would be hard to put anything over on Marla. "It's most likely a bounty hunter named Tulley," he admitted. "There might be a sheriff, too, but I don't think that's too likely. And it's been a long spell since a Texas Ranger got me in his sights."

"That's better, John. It's always the best policy to tell the truth."

"You sound like a schoolmarm," Slocum said. "Do you need a hand getting this stuff to the front door, Mrs. Johnson?"

"No, sir, Mr. Johnson, I don't. But I surely do thank you for the thought." Marla hefted her gear and lugged it to the front door. She knocked primly. Slocum didn't wait around to see what happened. Marla was more likely to get the room if the landlady thought she was renting to some farm family just passing through. One look at the worn but well-cared-for six-shooter stuck in the cross-draw holster and she'd know Slocum wasn't a sodbuster.

Slocum turned back for the town, the ten dollars Marla had given him burning a hole in his pocket. The warm beer he'd had—was it only three days back?—had whetted his thirst for real liquor. He wanted a shot of whiskey to cut the trail dust in his mouth. That he might have to go to several saloons before he found Vinson wasn't any problem, as far as Slocum could see.

Slocum dismounted and entered the Mesquite Saloon. He stood just inside the door and shook off the dust still clinging to him. He was glad he wore a canvas duster, but his clothes were still filthy. Slocum tried to figure out the best way of asking after Vinson when he heard a familiar voice from the rear of the saloon.

He had found Emmett Vinson in the very first saloon he tried. Slocum shook his head and laughed ruefully. He and Emmett always had the same tastes. Sometimes it was spooky. At others, it was downright frustrating.

"How much for a bottle of Billy Taylor's?" Slocum asked.

The barkeep looked up from under heavy lids. The man seemed well nigh asleep. The answer came slow and easy, "Fifty cents a shot, five dollars for the bottle. That's the better deal."

"You said it," Slocum said, counting out five one-dollar bills. Greenbacks weren't worth much to him. He preferred hard coin or even gold dust, but the barkeep took the bills without so much as a murmur.

Slocum grabbed a shot glass from the end of the bar as he made his way to the rear of the saloon. There he saw Emmett Vinson with his back in a corner. He was hunched forward, arguing with a frail man sitting with his back to the room.

Slocum wasn't superstitious, but aces and eights kept coming to mind. It was just good sense to keep your back to a wall when you were in a saloon. Even if no one in particular was gunning for you, it paid to watch everyone who came and went. That avoided a nasty spell of unexpected trouble.

Vinson glanced up when he saw Slocum approaching the

table. The man squinted and then smiled from ear to ear. "John! You made it! Come on, boy, sit down. Join us."

Slocum settled down beside Vinson, his back to a side of the saloon. He faced a high window and was able to see the others in the saloon reflected in it. Only when he was sure he could know what was going on around him did he turn his attention to the slight man Vinson had been talking to so intently.

"This here's Horace Wainwright," Vinson said. "John's one of my oldest friends. He'll be helping out."

Slocum didn't like what he saw in Wainwright. The man's nervous gestures were enough to make him tell Vinson to count him out. If this man had to stick a six-shooter under someone's nose in a robbery, he'd probably die of fright. Slocum demanded others in the robbery who were as businesslike as he was. Anything less was suicidal.

Horace Wainwright didn't look to be the robbing kind.

"Pleased, uh, John," Wainwright said. He obviously wanted to ask Slocum's last name but didn't have the guts to do it. Slocum silently saluted Vinson with his glass for this small victory. It didn't pay to have everyone in town know his name.

"Been on the trail a long time," Slocum said, savoring the smooth, hot flood of whiskey down his gullet. "Hate to be moving on so fast, but that's the way it looks."

"Now, John, don't go gettin' any ideas till you've heard the entire scheme," Vinson said.

Slocum knew that if he had a lick of sense he'd finish his whiskey, get up, and leave Grandville. There wasn't any amount of money worth risking his life for. Horace Wainwright was such an obvious weak link that Slocum wondered what had happened to Vinson's good sense.

Still, Slocum sat and talked with the two men. It took him a while to realize why: Marla Vinson. If she thought her brother had come up with a decent plan, the least Slocum could do was listen; and, he had to admit, the woman herself provided a powerful incentive to stick around just a spell longer.

5

Slocum's attention drifted as Emmett Vinson and the rabbity Horace Wainwright spoke in guarded tones. They were talking generalities that didn't interest him. Slocum wished Vinson would get down to telling what it was he intended to do in Grandville. This wasn't the kind of town Slocum enjoyed spending much time in.

He craned his neck and looked around the room. A few whores were drifting in for the evening trade, none of them particularly healthy looking. Upstairs would be the cribs and out back? Slocum guessed that the more incautious tipplers in the Mesquite Saloon would be clipped on the back of the skull by a club and their money taken if they strayed in that direction.

But where did the people of Grandville get the money to lose in a saloon like this? Ranching was the obvious answer, but the drought had sapped the countryside's wealth. Farming was out of the question without plentiful water. Even in the best of times, this dusty West Texas county didn't have enough for more than a small garden out back of a ranch house. Something supported so many saloons and gambling halls, and that was why Emmett Vinson was here. Slocum's attention eventually slipped back to the conversation between the other two men.

"So it looks damned good," Vinson said.

Wainwright's head bobbed as if it had been mounted on a spring. Slocum had the impression the man would agree to anything. Threaten to yell at him and he would lick your boots clean. If a robbery was like a chain, Horace Wainwright was the weakest link—or no link at all. Slocum had to decide.

"Let me give you one for the road, Horace," Vinson offered, using Slocum's bottle to do the pouring. The man knocked back the drink, his eyes huge behind wire-frame glasses thick enough to use for burning lenses. Wainwright gobbled something like a strangling bird and then almost ran from the saloon.

"So what do you think of our accomplice?" Vinson asked.

"This isn't the place to talk," Slocum said. In the plate glass window he had seen the reflections of two men. From the way they strutted in, they thought they were cocks of the walk. The gleaming badges pinned on their chests said they were deputies looking for someone's head to bash in.

"Those bully boys bother you?" Vinson laughed. "Don't let it. They're all blow and no go." In spite of his words, Vinson finished his drink in a rush and grabbed Slocum's bottle off the table. "Let's find a more private place."

"We've got a room out on the edge of town," Slocum said cautiously.

"We?"

"Marla and me," Slocum said, wondering how Emmett would take the fact that his sister was already in town and traveling with him.

"Good. Haven't seen Sis for too long. I'd sent her a down-the-wire telegram, just like the one I sent you, and hoped it would reach her. All I'd heard was that she had come to earth somewhere in Dallas."

Vinson walked past the two deputies without catching their eye. Slocum wasn't as lucky. They saw the way his six-shooter was slung; both of them turned slightly so their pistols would be ready for action. Slocum never broke stride as he walked past them. The hairs on the back of his neck rose as he left the saloon, wondering if they were reaching for their guns to shoot him in the back. He heaved a sigh of relief when he got outside.

"This is a peaceable enough town, John," Vinson told him. "The law doesn't go around looking for trouble."

"There're two deputies in one saloon," Slocum pointed out. "That means there's a sheriff and maybe other deputies. Why? There's no reason for Grandville to have that kind of police force."

Emmett Vinson took a swig from Slocum's bottle as they walked toward the rooming house. Slocum led his roan and Vinson grabbed the reins of a chestnut gelding. Slocum didn't bother asking if this was Vinson's horse. He knew the man was capable of such off-handed horse thievery, but he didn't think he would do it if a really big robbery was possible later.

"Ah, John, that's the beauty of it. There is money here. Lots of it. The railroad is coming in. The crew laying track is only fifteen miles outside town. They ought to be here inside a week and have a brand spanking new station built down the street a ways. It'll connect Grandville with the rest of the world."

"So there's money in the rail crew, but that's fifteen miles off," Slocum said.

"There's only one bank in Grandville." Vinson let this bit of information drift in the air to tantalize Slocum.

"That's where the railroad keeps its payroll?"

"Even better than that. There's a whale of a lot of money going into the bank right now because of the drought. The ranchers have to borrow heavily to keep going. The money's come in from another bank up north."

"How much money?"

"Always too eager, John, that's your problem. There's no telling how much money will be in the bank when we rob it because of something else. There's a long holiday coming up."

Slocum walked along, thinking hard. The railroad payroll was attractive enough, and the promise of a huge dollop of money from some northern bank just sitting and waiting for him to take it was a nice bonus. The notion that all the casinos and saloons in town might be stashing a long weekend's worth of revenue in the bank was even more appealing.

"It's not worth the risk," Slocum said suddenly.

"What? How can you say that, John? This is the robbery of the century. It'll go smooth as snot on glass. It's a natural for us!"

"Wainwright," said Slocum. "There's no way we can dance into a bank and expect him not to fold."

"He doesn't have to do a damned thing during the robbery," Vinson said, laughing. "It's hard enough for him to do anything now, but hatred and fear are powerful motivators."

"He works at the bank? He'll be an inside man?"

"Inside information, nothing more," Vinson assured him. "When we take the bank, there won't be anyone in it. I'm getting the information from poor Horace." Vinson chuckled. "He hates his boss so bad he'd do anything to get back at the bastard."

"The bank president?"

"President, owner, and tyrant," Vinson said with real satisfaction. "Marcus Bergstrom is his name and he's one royal son of a bitch, the kind of banker who'd foreclose on his widowed grandmother if there was a dime in it."

"What's Wainwright's cut?"

"Satisfaction," Vinson said. "He's doing this for revenge. He wants to see Bergstrom ruined. The old man makes his life hell."

"He'll end up losing his job if the bank goes under. Why doesn't Wainwright just up and quit if this Bergstrom is so bad?"

"That's you thinking and me thinking. Horace isn't like that. He's a frightened rabbit, a meek little mouse, the kind who lets others do his dirty work for him."

"He's the kind who'd be polite to your face and then shoot you in the back if the chance presented itself," Slocum said wearily. He'd come across men like Horace Wainwright before. He wasn't sure if the sheriff back in the no-name town he had just left wasn't like that.

"It's a sweet deal, John. Come on, let's find Marla and we can discuss it over the rest of this here bottle." Vinson held up Slocum's bottle. Less than half the fiery whiskey remained.

"Marla said she was registering under the name of Johnson," said Slocum.

"Smart girl. She knows better than to leave a trail. No need to give the law any chance to track us, if they do catch on. The beauty of the plan is that we can be long gone before they even twig to the robbery. Yes sir, this is one sweet plan."

Slocum left Vinson drinking and telling himself how great the robbery would be while he went inside the simple house.

"Yes?" came the sharp inquiry from a huge woman in the sitting room. "What can I do for you?"

"My wife, ma'am," Slocum said, tipping his dusty hat in her direction. "She checked in earlier. Mrs. Johnson?"

"Oh, yes, she said you'd be along after you finished your carousing." The woman's upper lip curled in disdain when she smelled the whiskey. "Dinner's in one hour sharp. I don't hold it for anybody. Be there or miss it."

"Yes, ma'am," Slocum said. He trudged up the stairs to the room Marla had rented. He opened the door and found himself with an armful of woman. Marla kissed him and then pushed back when he didn't return the passion.

"What's wrong, John? Don't you like the place?"

"It's fine." Slocum couldn't put what he felt into words. The robbery Emmett Vinson outlined didn't feel right to him. He had half a mind to just move on and let Vinson pull the heist without him, but he was afraid Marla would stay with her brother. He found himself wanting to be with her more than he wanted gold coins jingling in his pocket.

"John, did the bounty hunter find you?"

"Nothing like that," Slocum said. "I found Emmett in a saloon. He's outside waiting to talk to us."

"That's wonderful!" Marla rushed to the window and heaved it open. The gust of hot air that came in dried the sweat on Slocum's face. "Emmett, can you climb up?"

Slocum heard rustling noises. In a few seconds Emmett Vinson scrambled through the window and tumbled into the room. He sat on the floor, whiskey bottle in hand letting his sister kiss him.

"Enough of this mush," Emmett finally said. "It's good to see you, Sis. Glad you could get to Grandville for the biggest—"

"Robbery of the century," Slocum finished for him. He looked at Marla.

She caught his tone and was instantly wary.

"You need to tell me a lot more about the bank and the others involved before I'm in," Slocum added.

"But John, Emmett's doing the planning. You always said—"

"I always said Emmett was a good planner, but sometimes he gets too wild for his own good—or ours. A bank with that much money is going to have guards. If Bergstrom is as tight-fisted as he sounds, he might be sitting in the bank with a shotgun waiting for a robbery."

"He's a skinflint all right," Vinson said, sitting on the single bed. If he noticed Slocum's gear stacked with his sister's, he said nothing about it. "He can't keep guards because he refuses to pay them a fair wage. He depends on the town's sheriff to keep patrols moving past the bank."

"And with the number of deputies they seem to have in Grandville, that'd be pretty durn often," Slocum said.

"It is. I've watched. On a regular night, they pass the bank four or five times. Next weekend, they're likely to check the bank every half hour all night long."

"I think John has a point, Emmett," the woman said. "There's no way we could break in and blow the vault without having a passel of lawmen come down on us."

"Who else is involved?" asked Slocum.

Emmett Vinson held up his hand. "Whoa! Let me go over this. If there are questions, ask them then. I haven't come close to telling you the genius of this scheme." He took a long drink and then passed the bottle to Marla. She took a tentative sip, approved, and drank deeply. Slocum ended up with a bottle with only a few ounces left, but this was fine with him. He wanted a clear head when he argued the details with Vinson.

"The railroad's payroll will sit in the bank all weekend since Friday is a holiday and the railroad won't pay until the next banking day. The money from up north has been sitting there for some time. Bergstrom is too tight-fisted to dole it out without getting top dollar back. And the casinos will be dropping their receipts into the bank through a night depository slot; it goes right into the vault."

"The vault won't be opened until Monday morning?" asked Slocum.

"That's right. So we hit it Sunday night."

"We can't blow it, Emmett. You just said—" Marla clamped her mouth shut when her shot her a cold look.

"We don't blow it. We don't even have to break in. Some yahoo honeycombed the area under the town with tunnels. Who knows what he was looking for, but he never found it—and it took years."

"Tunnels?"

"Mine shafts, everywhere under Grandville. I've heard old man Proctor was looking for lead or tin or some such. Piss-poor area for that. He burrowed like a prairie dog for years until he gave up. Grandville grew up about then. The tunnels are everywhere—including under the bank. We might have to do a bit of tunneling of our own, but not much."

"So we come up under the vault?" Slocum liked this better and better, but it was a whale of a lot of work.

"Wouldn't do much good," said Vinson. He leaned forward, hands on his knees. His face flushed with excitement. "There's two solid inches of iron on all sides of that vault, and that includes the bottom. No, we break into the bank and just open the vault as slick as you please."

Slocum began to understand. "Wainwright gave you the combination."

"Yes! We have the combination and we open the vault and leave through the tunnels. The sheriff will never see us. By the time Bergstrom opens the vault at nine the next morning, we'd have a night's travel behind us."

"Who else is going to be in on this?" Slocum asked. He still didn't like Wainwright's participation. He was a weak sister. He would betray them if any pressure was put on him.

"That's the real beauty of the plan, John. We're going to do it ourselves. Just the three of us. Marla can act as lookout while you and I get the loot."

"And then there's Wainwright," Slocum said, still not liking the bank teller's part in the robbery.

"There's always Wainwright, but he'll have something more precious than gold. He'll have the satisfaction of seeing his boss's bank picked clean."

Emmett Vinson made a good argument for a quick and profitable robbery. Slocum looked at Marla and saw that she was behind her brother one hundred percent. He felt his resolve to just ride on out of Grandville wavering.

"Count me in, Emmett," he heard himself saying. He damned himself for being such a fool. Slocum knew it wasn't for the money he was taking part. It was to be with Marla Vinson.

6

"This place is good enough to keep as a base, but it's too far away from the action to do us much good during the robbery," Slocum said. The boardinghouse's landlady also posed a threat to their bank robbery plans. She kept an eagle eye on Slocum, not trusting him. The woman had yet to come right out and ask if he and Marla were really married. Such bluntness would be a breach of etiquette, but the woman obviously had her suspicions. It wouldn't do to goad her into asking the town's sheriff to check on her illicit boarders.

Slocum knew that the wanted posters Tulley had might be circulating throughout West Texas. Even if they weren't, it wouldn't take much searching to turn up something on him. And Slocum had no idea what Emmett Vinson had been doing the past few years. He might be wanted in every state and territory west of the Mississippi. The only real chance they had of pulling off the robbery was to be quiet and not create much of a fuss.

"We need to look at the bank ourselves," Slocum said. He lounged on the soft feather bed, thinking it would be nice to have something like this under him every night. Marla was hanging clothing in the tall wooden wardrobe leaning against the opposite wall.

Just lying there and staring at her made Slocum think things that seldom crossed his mind. It was good with Marla Vinson, better than with any other woman he could remember. She had spunk and fire that most women lacked. And courage? She was stronger than most men. He couldn't help comparing her to Horace Wainwright. She had a moral fiber he lacked, even if she was helping to rob a bank.

Slocum didn't think that was too important a crime. The real crimes were cowardice and breaking your word. A man might lose any amount of money, but if he kept his honor, he was still a man. Slocum knew he could trust Marla with his life.

About Horace Wainwright he wasn't going to press the point. This wasn't a man to turn your back on.

"We can go to the bank on the pretense of opening an account," Marla suggested. "Who'd ever suspect a loving husband and wife?"

"The casinos aren't going to put any of their money into Bergstrom's bank over the weekend," Slocum said, his mind already on other matters. "There's not a saloon owner in the world who would trust a banker without facing him when the deposit was made."

"There's still the railroad payroll and the money from up north," Marla said. "That ought to be enough to split three ways."

"Even a thousand dollars total would make for a good weekend," Slocum said. He didn't like Emmett's idea of waiting until Sunday night to get into the bank. Better to strike Friday night. That would give them well nigh three days to get away. The weather might turn bad again. The dust hadn't blown in hours, but it could start up at any time.

Marla had the right idea coming up from Dallas: water. They needed a good supply of water before they hightailed it out of Grandville.

"What are you thinking about, John?" Marla turned and stared at him. She was dressed but hadn't buttoned the front of her dress. He couldn't keep from looking at the luscious divide between her breasts. He felt stirrings that had to be put aside for the moment. He needed to concentrate on the robbery.

"Hurry up. I want to get to the bank around noontime. It'll be busier then and we won't be as noticeable." He smiled crookedly as he studied her. "Then again, any time you went folks would notice you. The men would be wondering how to get to know you better and the women would be hating you for looking so good."

"I'll take that as a compliment," Marla said. She made no move to cover the bare flesh. She knew she was arousing Slocum and enjoyed it. After a few seconds, she turned and bent over, her softly rounded behind poking up into the air. It was all Slocum could do to keep from going to her.

Marla Vinson finished hunting for whatever it was in the bottom of the wardrobe and quickly put the final touches on her dress. She hesitated as she buttoned the top button. To leave it open would be an invitation to gossip.

"I do so hate hot weather," she said, fixing the last button at the hollow of her throat.

"We'll be able to head north and find cooler weather soon enough," Slocum said. "There ought to be enough money in that bank to keep us happy for a long time."

She smiled but didn't answer directly. Marla held out her arm and Slocum took it. He didn't like it, but he dropped his cross-draw holster on the bed before leaving the room. It wouldn't do to attract attention by wearing it into the bank.

As if they were a married couple out for a Sunday stroll, they made their way to the Grandville Bank at the corner of Main and Stodder. Slocum's sharp eyes studied the huge brick structure. Two stories high, it dominated the entire area. Heavy iron bars over the windows made it look more like a prison than a bank. The door into the lobby swung on rusty hinges—or so Slocum thought at first.

Entering the lobby, he saw that the hinges were overworked. The doors must have steel centers. Heavy locking bars dropped in to seal the front when the bank closed. Slocum wondered where Marcus Bergstrom's private entrance was. The bank president must leave through it every night after locking up.

He shook himself. They weren't coming in like ordinary bandits. They were going to come up through the floor. Slocum found himself walking slowly and staring at the heavy wood planking. If a mine shaft lay under the floor, he didn't hear the hollow ring as he walked. He didn't know if this was for the best or not. Surely someone would have noticed a hollow sound a long time back and told Bergstrom. Any tunnel would have been found and filled.

But if there wasn't any indication of a tunnel, how were they going to get into the bank?

Slocum glanced up and into the huge barrel of a shotgun. He threw up his hands and stepped back.

"Sorry, mister," said the guard. "Didn't recognize you, so I got orders to cover everybody."

"I just wanted to open an account. The wife and I are moving to Grandville. Maybe we ought to find another place."

"Like I said, I'm real sorry I spooked you. Go on over to the teller's cage."

"Let's go to another bank, dear," Marla said. "We are obviously not wanted here."

"There ain't another bank in these parts," the guard said. He turned slightly when a bulky man with a florid face came bustling from a back office. "Oh, shit, I'm in for it now," the guard muttered. "That's Mr. Bergstrom, the bank president."

"What's going on?" the man demanded. Slocum wasn't sure if Bergstrom was asking the guard or him.

"We wanted to open a savings account," Marla said smoothly, unfazed by the shotgun. She saw how Slocum had bristled instantly upon seeing the man. "There seems to be some problem." She touched the muzzle of the shotgun and pushed it away.

"There's no problem. If you want to open an account, see one of the tellers. Why are you bothering me? None of you have the sense God gave a bird." Bergstrom harumped, spat at a brass cuspidor, and missed. He swung around and went back to his office.

"Leastwise, he didn't fire me. I surely am sorry about this. Getting the drop on anybody I don't know is what he told me to do, honest."

"I can believe that," Slocum said. "Come on. Let's get on with our business." Slocum saw that the only teller available of the three behind iron cages was Horace Wainwright. Slocum turned and said to Marla, "You do the work."

She nodded and went to the window, speaking with Wainwright in a low voice. Slocum stood with his back to the man. He didn't want the teller to associate Marla with him. It hadn't been good meeting in the saloon the way they had. Slocum would have preferred never knowing about Wainwright or having the man be able to identify him.

"There, dear, it's all done," Marla said, tucking a small book into her purse. "We opened an account for eight dollars, the bank's minimum. We shall receive one percent interest on the money, paid twice a year."

"All we need is to be paid once," Slocum said. Marla laughed, knowing what he meant. They were going to make a withdrawal, and it wasn't going to be just eight dollars.

Outside, Slocum heaved a sigh of relief. The bank's interior had made him feel imprisoned. He didn't regret having gone inside, though, he needed to know the layout before they broke in.

"Learn what you needed?" Marla asked.

"I got enough to be happy. The flooring seems mighty substantial, though. I hope Emmett's not blowing smoke about those mine tunnels."

"He knows what he's doing," Marla said. "Now we need to find a place for me to keep watch. That's not going to be too easy. The bank's about all there is around here unless I go to the roof of that building." She pointed to an adjoining yard goods store.

"The hotel down the block might be good enough if you took a room on the third floor. You could see the street from a front room."

"I don't know," she said. "I could only see Stodder. There isn't a view of Main Street from there, even if I leaned out the window."

"There might be. Let's go see," Slocum said. The area around the Grandville Bank wasn't built up as much as the hotel. There might be a view of the main street—not a good one but enough for their purposes. All Marla had to do was alert them to anyone trying to get in. If she could see the front doors and Bergstrom's private entrance, that would be good enough.

They walked into the shabby hotel lobby. The once-proud carpeting was threadbare and the stairs leading to the upper stories looked as if they would collapse under their own weight. But Slocum wasn't interested in quality. He wanted a room with a good view for Marla. He wasn't going into the

Grandville Bank without someone on the outside he trusted to warn him if things turned sour.

"How long?" the bored clerk asked.

"The wife and me'll be putting up for about a week," Slocum said. "Reckon it'll take that long to find work. Heard tell the railroad's about ready to come into town."

"Next month there'll be a new station. You a railroad man?"

"That I am," Slocum lied.

The clerk, after a little haggling, gave them a room on the top floor overlooking the street. They trudged up the stairs and went into the room. Slocum closed and locked the door.

"How's it look?" he asked.

Marla opened the window and leaned out. She took her time making the appraisal. "It'll be fine, John. I can see the front doors and that green awning must shelter the door where Bergstrom comes and goes. It's not great, but I can see it."

"We're all set then," he said, sitting on the hard bed. "All we need to do is check the tunnels and get ready for this weekend." His mind turned to the date of the robbery. He would have to talk Emmett out of robbing the bank Sunday. Friday was safer. That would give them plenty of time to get away.

Slocum smiled at the idea of going to the railhead and taking the train to who knows where it started. Rob the railroad company and then use their very own train to escape. The idea appealed to him.

Marla sat on the bed and asked, "A penny for your thoughts."

The top buttons had come undone on her dress—or perhaps she had loosened them just for him.

"I was thinking it's a shame to waste this room. We've

got the place at the boardinghouse, but we've still paid for this room for a week."

"It's not a great bed," Marla said, bouncing on it. As she moved up and down, Slocum found himself watching the movement under her dress. Her breasts jiggled enough to make him think of how they could get their money's worth out of the room.

He bent over and kissed her. She sank back to the bed, her fingers lacing through his black hair. Slocum moved fully onto the bed and said, "I'm glad I didn't wear my gun belt. It'd only be in the way."

"I feel something hard," Marla said.

"Damn," he said, sitting up. He fumbled in his vest pocket and pulled out the derringer he had brought instead of his Colt Navy. Slocum put it on the small table beside the bed. "There, that ought to take care of the problem."

"That wasn't what I felt, and it's not a problem." Marla squeezed down harder at his crotch. Slocum groaned softly as she began kneading the rigid length she had found. She took a special glee in stroking and then pressing hard. Slocum didn't utter a word. If he had, he would have simply demanded more from the lovely Marla.

Slocum rolled onto his back and let the woman slowly undress him. Then it was his turn. The dress opened and revealed her full charms. He kissed her throat, to her shoulders, and then down until he found a succulent mound of female flesh. His tongue licked and teased until the nipple atop the firm white hillock was hot, hard, and pulsing with her passion.

Marla gasped, "John, I'm burning up inside. Do something about it. Please, now, I can't wait!"

He skinned the dress off her, relishing the sight of her long legs slipping free. Those legs parted for him as he moved closer. His hips worked back and forth and suddenly he found the center of her being. He was completely surrounded and felt as if he were being sucked in. Moist and hot, she clung to his lusty, hard length.

"That's what I need, John. That's exactly what I need," she cooed. Marla lay on the bed, her head tossed back, her dark hair spread over the pillow in wild disarray. Slocum wondered if he had ever seen a more beautiful woman. He didn't think so.

He began moving, slowly at first and then with greater speed and power. The fire in his loins demanded quenching. He tried to ram deeper into her with each thrust of his hips, and each time she yielded and flowed away. The heat mounted and burned at him with a carnal fire that he couldn't deny.

"Now, John, now!" she cried.

She clung to him, lifting herself partially off the bed. Her fingernails dug into his shoulders and her entire body shook like a leaf in a high wind. A hot flush rose, engulfing her breasts and shoulders. Then Slocum was past noticing such intimate details. His balls tightened and he exploded into her gripping interior.

Slocum gasped and rode out the tornado of desire that blew through him. Spent, he sank down atop the woman and focused once more on her loveliness. Marla Vinson seemed to glow with an inner light that made her even more beautiful.

"I like being your lookout," Marla said. Her arms circled him and pulled him close. "I like being with you," she finished with a sigh. She rested her head on his shoulder. He felt her soft breath gusting through the hair on his bare chest.

Slocum had to admit that teaming up with Emmett Vinson had brought unexpected benefits. He hoped the robbery would go as smoothly as everything else had so far.

7

Slocum and Marla Vinson left the hotel after making love for a second time. He paused when they reached the street. It was past noon and already the saloons were starting to fill.

"Do you want to take another look around the town, John?" she asked. She smiled knowingly and gave his arm a squeeze and said, "I'll be back at the boardinghouse waiting for you. I'll tell the old busybody that you're out looking for work."

"Be careful what you say," Slocum cautioned. "She might know somebody who needs a hand right about now. Grandville looks to be a boomtown and hired help might be hard to find."

"I'll tell her you're thinking about taking a job, then, but I'll be vague about where. Is that all right?"

"You know it is," Slocum said. He kissed her lightly and then looked around to see if anyone was watching. It wasn't proper to kiss a decent woman in public like that. Folks might get to thinking Marla was a whore, or at least a loose woman. Slocum didn't want to get into a fight over that, because people would die for sure.

"Always the cautious one. Emmett thinks you're some kind of crazy man always taking unnecessary risks, but you're not. You're about the most patient and thoughtful man I've ever seen."

·"Think of me and then think of the cougar waiting all day for his prey to come along before he pounces," Slocum said. His mind was already halfway down Main Street. The bustle of the casinos drew him, and he still had five dollars of Marla's money in his pocket.

"Be careful. Don't forget that you left your six-shooter back at the boardinghouse."

Slocum touched his vest pocket where the derringer rode like a small, hard fist. He smiled at Marla to reassure her that he wouldn't do anything foolish. With an entire bank vault loaded with money just waiting for them to take this weekend, he wasn't about to get into any trouble.

Marla turned and walked off. Slocum stood and watched her as she gracefully made her way down the boardwalk and went toward a dry goods store. She stopped to look at the dress in the window, then entered the store. In her own way she was casing the town. Slocum felt he had to do the same, in his own way.

The first saloon he entered was dim, dank, and smelled of stale beer. The sawdust on the floor hadn't been swept out in a coon's age and the barkeep leaning against the rickety bar moved more slowly than any man Slocum had seen this side of the grave.

"What's your pleasure?" the barkeep finally asked.

"Beer," Slocum said, not wanting to spend more of his five dollars than he had to. The mug of warm beer cost him the lone nickel he had left over from his trip into Grandville. Somehow, spending it made him feel as if he had made a clean break with the past. All the troubles he had endured over the past few weeks were gone with the silver coin. And the crisp five dollar greenback marked the start of a bright and profitable future.

"Why's everyone in town in the middle of the week?" Slocum asked.

"Getting ready for the big celebration this weekend." When he saw that Slocum didn't know what the big celebration was about, he added in a scornful tone, "San Jacinto Day. That's when—"

"General Houston defeated the Mexicans back in '36," Slocum finished for him. He had known, but it had slipped his mind. This had been a point he had intended asking Emmett Vinson about: What was the occasion for the bank holiday? Now that he knew, another piece of the puzzle fell nicely into place. This whole scheme wasn't Emmett Vinson blowing smoke. It was a for-sure celebration. Slocum had been around other Texas towns and had seen how they celebrated. Sometimes the drinking and carousing went on for a week.

"We've been lookin' forward to this for months," the barkeep said. He swung a dirty dishrag around and around. Slocum wondered if he was going to polish glasses with it or mop the floor. From its appearance, the barkeep might have done both already.

"Bank's closing down, is it?" Slocum asked.

"On Friday. Galls that son of a bitch banker man no end, but he's coming out ahead doing it."

"Oh? How's that?" Slocum sipped at his beer and wondered what the metallic undertaste was. It burned his tongue rather than going down smooth.

"The railroad's made a deal with Bergstrom since Friday is the twenty-first. They don't want their men coming into town and spendin' their entire paycheck in one night, so

Bergstrom's keeping their payroll until the following Monday."

"He's a man who likes to look at a pile of money?"

The barkeep snorted. "He owns damned near everything in this town from the land the bank's built on out to the cemetery. Heard tell he doesn't own that because he's so damned superstitious, but he owns the undertaking parlor across the street. Anything for a penny, that's Marcus Bergstrom."

"A fine, upstanding man," Slocum said. He didn't bother finishing the beer. The barkeep raised an eyebrow and indicated the mug. When Slocum motioned for him to take it away, the bartender dumped it back into the keg he had drawn it from.

"Waste not, want not," the barkeep said.

Slocum had to agree, even if the small amount of information he'd received and the mouthful of warm beer was hardly worth a nickel.

He walked down the street until he came to the general store. An old man sat on the boardwalk, his chair tipped back against the wall by the pickle barrel, whittling away.

"Mind if I set a spell with you?" Slocum asked, perching on the edge of the walk.

"Free country, leastwise that's what they try to tell us." The old codger eyed Slocum, one eye squinting and the other a bit on the rheumy side. "Haven't seen you around town before. You with the railroad?"

"Hope to be," Slocum said. He still liked the idea of riding to the railhead and taking the train come Saturday morning and being hundreds of miles away before the bank opened for business on Monday. He'd miss the San Jacinto celebration, but that was a small price to pay for a vault filled with money.

"They's flocking to Grandville to work for the damn railroad," the old man said. He spat a gob of tobacco into the street and went back to his whittling. "Not doin' this town one bit of good."

"Why's that? More people means more money. Everyone prospers."

"Sinful gains, that's what it is. Look at them saloons. Ten more'n there was this time last year. And gambling. You can't believe what goes on in there."

Slocum eyed the old man and said carefully, "You could have fooled me. I'd've taken you for the gambling sort."

The man snorted and nodded. "When I was younger, but now I know better. Hell, son, when I was about your age I actually tried mining this land. Can you believe it?"

"Mining? For gold?"

"Not gold," the old man said. "Grandville started as a hope and prayer that there was tin under these hills."

Slocum started to ask what hills and then stopped. For someone born and bred in West Texas, the rolling prairie might be considered hills. To him, the Sierra Madres were real peaks. These were hardly pimples on the face of the land.

"Tried mining for years, I did. Me and a dozen others like that crazy son of a bitch Proctor. We cut tunnels through this place until you couldn't walk without falling into one of our holes." The old man shook his head. "Those were good days."

"But you didn't find any tin," Slocum said.

"The dream's what counts, son, not the achieving. If we'd found the tin it would be us over there in that fancy brick bank and not Mr. Marcus Bergstrom."

Slocum noted that no one in Grandville seemed too fond of the banker. That suited him fine. It would be that much harder for the bank owner to get a posse together—unless he convinced the townspeople that it was their money that had been stolen. Then no amount of hatred for the banker would keep the good people of Grandville from hunting down the swine who'd robbed their bank.

"Exciting times back then, I reckon," said Slocum. "What happened to the tunnels? I suppose they were some distance away from where the town got built."

"Some were, some weren't. Haven't much thought about the mines for a spell," the old coot said. "Been thinking about the celebration coming up. They're having a parade and band and everything. Brings too many people to town, I say."

Slocum slipped away, leaving the old man muttering to himself about the railroad and progress and how it was ruining a perfectly good town. Slocum was pleased with himself. He had verified much of what Emmett had told him. The mine shafts did exist, and maybe they ran under the town itself. That was something Slocum would have to check out later. Now, he was more interested in finding a small poker game and parlaying his money into a bigger poke.

After looking into several casinos and judging the crowd inside, Slocum finally chose the Lucky Dice Saloon and Gaming Hall. The men inside were ranch hands and didn't appear to know the odds in stud poker anywhere near as well as Slocum.

He found himself in a penny-ante game, which suited him just fine. A few hands later he had doubled his stake and was ready to move on.

"Wait a minute, mister," said the man across the table from him. "You're leaving with damn near a dollar of my money. At least give me a couple hands to try to win it back."

Slocum was aware of the lack of bulk on his left hip where his Colt Navy usually hung. All he had was the derringer in his pocket. It was a big caliber and had the wallop of a mule's kick, but it wasn't anywhere near as accurate as the Colt.

Worse, it held only two rounds. Slocum saw that the others in the game agreed with the man who was complaining.

A strategic retreat might be in order, he decided. All he had to do was lose a few dollars back and everyone would be happy.

"Deal," he said. "Seven card or five?"

Slocum bet carefully, intending to lose. The hands consistently went in his direction. It was hard to fold when three of the cards showing were queens. The best anyone else at the table had was a pair of deuces. Even when he could fold and not look to be a quitter, Slocum didn't lose that much.

"Are you cheatin'?" the cowboy asked. The level tone put Slocum on his guard. If there had been anger, he might have been able to jolly the man a bit with a drink and smooth things over. But the cowboy sounded as if he wanted a serious fight.

"Don't have to with the luck I've had today," Slocum said. "And there's no need to cheat you with the poor luck you've been having. These are house cards and the rest of you have been doing most of the dealing."

"It's just a bad day, Roy. I been watching him like a hawk and he ain't cheated you once." The man to Slocum's left scratched his stubbly chin and leaned forward. "And I been watchin' you, too," he said to the man to Slocum's right. "That's a mighty convincing set of hole cards you've got up your sleeve."

The man lurched across Slocum, grabbed the cowboy's arm, and jerked hard. The cowboy fell forward, sending chips and cards flying. Slocum managed to wiggle back. His hand drifted for the derringer but he saw that it wasn't needed.

"You been tryin' to cheat and you've done a piss-poor job of it, you stupid galoot," the one named Roy said. Slocum tried to figure out what was going on. Apparently the others in the game, maybe Roy and the man caught cheating, were in cahoots.

"Damned poor job," said the man who had been on Slocum's left. "They didn't even win."

Slocum recreated the deal and saw what had happened. Roy and his partner had been off by one hand all afternoon. They had been giving Slocum the cards rather than dealing them to each other. At this he had to laugh. He had been cheated before by some of the best, but this was the first time he had been helped out by accident.

"Don't reckon I ought to keep this money if they were cheating," Slocum said. "Bartender, drinks for everyone at this table until the money's gone." He slapped down four singles and some change. With luck he might be able to walk away with almost a seventy-five cent gain from the game. It wasn't what he'd intended, but it was better than leaving hard feelings.

"That's mighty kind of you, mister. I think I'd just as soon string these two cheating cayuses up by their necks."

Slocum edged away, not wanting to get involved. Out of the corner of his eye he saw the saloon door open and close. For a moment he wondered what it was about the man who entered that had caught his attention. Men had come and gone from the Lucky Dice all afternoon.

Then Slocum turned and got a better look. The bounty hunter almost completely filled the door, his huge bulk blocking out the bright sunlight. Slocum saw that Tulley limped a mite. He reckoned his bullet had caught him in the thigh and that it wasn't much of a wound. It might slow the bounty hunter a bit, but it hadn't come anywhere near stopping him.

Slocum turned back to the cowhands wrangling over the game. They had come to an agreement of sorts and were beginning to drink from the liquor Slocum had purchased.

A quick flash of anger passed through Slocum. He wasn't sure if he hadn't been had by some playacting. These men surely did look friendly all of a sudden.

Tulley had ordered his whiskey and was turning to survey everyone in the room. He couldn't miss Slocum unless he had gone blind out in the sun. Slocum touched the derringer again and knew it wouldn't be much good against the huge bounty hunter. And he also knew he wasn't up to a fistfight with the mountain of gristle. Anything that attracted the law was likely to cause the robbery to be canceled.

Slocum had already started thinking about how he'd spend his share of the loot. He wasn't going to let the bounty hunter ruin the sweetest deal he'd seen in years.

Slocum reached out and grabbed Roy by the shirt and pulled him halfway across the table. "You're one cheating son of a bitch. I ought to see you strung up."

"Wha—" Roy sputtered. And, as Slocum had already guessed, the others came to his aid. Slocum slipped under a punch and landed a hard right in the center of a stomach. He didn't even see who he hit. And it didn't matter. The cowboys all piled on, and Slocum dived under the table.

The fight raged above as he crawled away. He got to the saloon's back door and pulled himself erect. His trick had worked. Tulley was cheering Roy on as he fought with two others from the next table who had joined in. The bounty hunter's attention had been diverted enough so that he'd never know Slocum was in town.

The robbery might just come off, but Tulley's presence in Grandville made it more dangerous than it had been.

8

"I don't like the looks of this, Emmett." Slocum walked bent over double as he examined the old mine tunnels that had been cut through the hard caprock. "These timbers haven't been shored up in years. Dry rot has set in—or termites. I can't tell which from the condition of the wood." Slocum ran his fingers over one roof beam and came away with a handful of powdery wood. He brushed it off on his trousers. Trying to move in the tunnels was bad enough; having them collapse while they were inside was something he didn't want to consider.

Slocum shuddered at the idea of being buried alive. That fear was one reason he didn't work much in mines. He wasn't afraid of closed-in places, but being underground was different. The notion that tons of dirt might come crashing down on his head made him uneasy.

"They'll hold, John. I do declare, you worry more than any two men I ever met." Emmett Vinson held a carbide light to illuminate their path. "This tunnel goes straight for the heart of Grandville. I tried to figure where to start digging up to get into the bank. See if you don't agree with the spot I chose."

Slocum grumbled to himself as they worked their way along the stope. The things he did for a quick buck.

"Here, here it is," said Vinson, stopping and pointing to a spot in the roof he had marked with a large white chalk X. "I reckon this will bring us up right under the bank's lobby."

Slocum tried to determine their location by his tracking sense. It was hard to get so turned around he didn't know what direction he traveled. Underground things weren't measured by left or right or north and south but by degrees. He had tried to keep track of the twists and turns in the shaft.

"This doesn't feel right," he said. "We're too far south of the bank. It ought to be more in that direction." He pointed down a crossing tunnel.

"We can dig up and see what's there," suggested Vinson. "Of course, if I'm right, we'll come up in the middle of a bunch of frightened depositors."

Slocum sat cross-legged on the ground and tried to figure out if his sense of direction had played him wrong. He didn't think so. If they dug straight up here, they'd end up in a lot down the street from the bank. Other than digging and seeing what was there, he didn't know any way of proving Emmett right or wrong.

"What if we drilled a small hole and stuck a wire up it," Slocum suggested, the idea coming to him slowly. "Not too long a wire but enough for us to see."

"There's wood planking in the bank. We'd have to drill through it, too."

"If we hit wood, I'll buy you a drink and agree that you're right on the money."

Vinson laughed at this small joke. "John, I hate taking your money like that, but it's a deal. I've spent more'n a week choosing this spot. It's right."

"Let's drill," Slocum said. They got out a hand drill and took turns holding it against the rocky mine roof. Slocum was guiding it and Vinson turning the gears to give the drill some speed when the bit broke through and sent a cascade of dust and rock down on them. Slocum backed off immediately.

"No wood chips or sawdust," he said, looking through the debris he'd brought down. "Hand me that wire. I'll push it through, then we'll go looking for where it comes out. Let's hope it's not in the middle of the sheriff's office."

"You're getting down in the mouth in your old age, John. You always were impetuous. Let's see some of that now. We need to believe things are just fine." Emmett Vinson worked to straighten a length of baling wire. When he had a seven-foot length, he fastened a piece of dirty white rag on the end loop and started feeding it through the hole Slocum had drilled.

"There," he said. "The tip of the wire is poking out. It feels different from when I was pushing it through the hole."

Slocum brushed the dirt from his face and hands. "Let's get into Grandville and find it. A drink says the wire's sticking up in the empty lot behind the bank. We'll have to drill from over there to reach the bank lobby."

"Christ, John, let's hope that's not so," said Vinson. "The rock's extra hard there. This stuff is like cheese. Over there—" He shook his head as if saying it was an impossible task.

They left the mine and Slocum heaved a sigh of relief when the hot West Texas sun slashed at his face. He hadn't enjoyed being out in it before. He knew now that there were worse places to spend his life. Being a prairie dog wasn't to his liking. He and Vinson got on their horses and rode the mile or more back into Grandville.

"You're mighty quiet, John. Is anything wrong?"

Slocum had been considering what to do about the bounty hunter. Tulley was a problem he had to solve on his own. He didn't want Emmett knowing he had trouble sniffing at his heels. He would be likely to call off the robbery. For all his talk of daring, Emmett Vinson occasionally showed a spark of good sense. Waiting until after the bounty hunter was taken care of fell into that slot.

Slocum wanted the money from the bank and he wanted to be as far away from Grandville as he could get. It was Wednesday, and in two days, if he could convince Vinson to move up the robbery from Sunday night, they'd be on their way with more money than they had any right to.

"Nothing's wrong. I was just wondering if we could blast a mite before getting down to the drilling. It might make the work a damn sight less."

"There's no need," Vinson assured him. "The wire is poking up inside the bank. I tell you, I checked it out a dozen times. I measured. I paced it off underground. I made damned sure it was right."

Slocum knew Emmett was blowing smoke out his ass then. There was no way to pace off anything in the cramped tunnels. They couldn't even stand up straight, much less march off a decent interval. He let the slight exaggeration ride. There would be time later to correct his friend's mistake, but it would take a considerable amount of work. Slocum wondered if they shouldn't start digging right now if they wanted to be through by Friday night.

"About the timing on this robbery, Emmett," Slocum said. "There's not going to be that much added to the bank's stash over the weekend. The casinos and saloons have guards of their own. They might deposit their revenues on Monday, but it would be too late to get the railroad payroll if we waited till Monday night."

"What are you saying?"

"Let's take the bank Friday night. That'd give us the entire weekend to hightail it out of here."

"But there'd be so much more," Vinson protested. "The holiday revenues from the saloons! It's a young fortune, John. We can use that money just as good as they can."

"It's not worth it, Emmett. The railroad payroll and the money from up north are what make this interesting. The money from the gambling is just icing on the cake. I want the cake—all of it."

"Maybe you're right, John. I'll have to think on it a spell," he said. "Right now we got to meet with Horace. He left a note over at the stable for me saying there was something important he had to discuss."

This put Slocum on his guard. "Did he mention what it was? Has something gone haywire?"

"I reckon we'll have to ask him personal-like. He wanted to have a drink over at the Mesquite Saloon. You want to join us or are you still keepin' apart?"

"I'll join you," Slocum said, coming to a fast decision. He wanted to hear Wainwright's excuses with his own ears. Vinson wanted this robbery to happen in the worst way. He might miss a double-cross in the works. Slocum wanted the money from the bank but not if it meant sticking his neck into a hangman's noose. He had troubles enough with Tulley on his trail.

They entered the saloon through a side door. Slocum looked around and made sure the bounty hunter wasn't anywhere to be seen. Only then did he settle into a chair with his back to a wall. Vinson took a chair beside him and ordered two shots of whiskey. By the time the liquor had been slopped down in front of them, the mousy bank teller had poked his nose through the door and was looking around.

Vinson signaled. Wainwright hurried over and quickly sat, as if the mere act of sitting made him invisible to the rest of the men in the saloon. He gave every impression of not wanting to be seen. Slocum wondered why he hadn't picked a more private spot.

"Afternoon, Horace. Is everything going well with you?" Vinson hoisted his drink and sipped at it in greeting. Slocum noticed he didn't offer the teller a drink. Slocum sat back and decided to listen rather than put his two cents in.

"Afternoon, Mr. Vinson." The teller looked furtive. Slocum compared this with the way he had been at their first meeting. Then he had been both frightened and bold. He was getting back at his employer, was scared of doing it, and was feeling his oats, nonetheless. But now? Slocum couldn't put a name to what he saw in the man.

"We've got problems, Mr. Vinson," Wainwright went on. "Bergstrom is making me work Saturday. I've got to balance all the accounts and I'm not sure I can do it in just one day. It might take me too."

"So?" Vinson's eyebrow arched just enough to show he wanted Wainwright to spell out the problem.

"You said I wouldn't be on the premises when you busted in."

"That's right."

"I might be working Saturday night and maybe Sunday, during the day, too."

"That's no problem, is it, John?" Vinson addressed Slocum but his eyes never left Horace Wainwright. "We're planning on blowing the bank open Sunday night, after all the casinos make their deposits through that fancy armored slot Bergstrom installed in his vault."

"I just don't want to be there. He'd know I had something to do with it if you broke in and then opened the vault using the combination."

"Why won't Bergstrom suspect you anyway?" asked Slocum. "How many people know the combination?"

"Just Mr. Bergstrom," came the immediate answer. "He doesn't know I learned it. I—I saw it on a slip of paper when the vault was installed."

"I see," said Vinson. "You think if we blasted in while you were there, then used the combination, Bergstrom would especially blame you. That's a fair concern, isn't it, John?"

"Reckon so," Slocum allowed. "We'll just have to be sure Horace is out of the bank."

"I'll be done by Sunday, I know it, I know it," the man said. Again Slocum heard the furtiveness in his voice—and something else. There was more than a touch of fear, too.

"Count on us, Horace. You've done well. We'll do right by you. You have my promise." Vinson leaned across the table and shook Wainwright's limp hand.

"Thank you, Mr. Vinson. I knew I could count on you. Thank you, thank you." Horace Wainwright spun out of his chair and scuttled off like a small mouse. He didn't even look behind him as he darted through the door and out into Main Street.

"What do you make of that, John?" Vinson knocked back the last of his whiskey.

"I don't like it. He's getting cold feet. We ought to make our move Friday night or not at all."

"You have a good point. Friday's lookin' better'n better to me all the time. Let's go see if we can find a wire stickin' up somewhere. That'll tell us how much work we've got ahead."

"Then you can buy me another drink. Scooting around in those mines made me work up a powerful thirst," Slocum said.

They left the Mesquite Saloon and circled the huge structure, coming out on the street running behind the bank. They hiked a few blocks and then stopped. Vinson looked toward the bank. Slocum was looking in the other direction, scanning the weed-infested lot just behind the brick bank building.

"There's about where the wire ought to be," said Vinson, pointing to the southeast corner of the bank. "Can't be more'n a few feet to the lobby."

"And this is where the wire actually came through," said Slocum. He kicked through the sand and exposed the bent tip of a piece of baling wire.

"That's not the same one, John. Don't kid a kidder."

Slocum tugged until he had seven feet of wire pulled out of the ground. At the end was tied a small piece of white rag.

"Look familiar?"

"I owe you a drink. And you were right about where we have to dig. Damnation! How could I have been so far off?"

Vinson threw his hat to the ground and stood, hands on hips, shaking his head. Slocum had to admit it was a good thing that the man was able to admit he had been wrong. They would have tunneled up and into an empty stretch of land.

"We'll have to do a passel more work than I intended," Vinson said. "I'd better be sure we've got picks and shovels for it. I'll pay you the drink later, John." Emmett Vinson went off muttering to himself.

Slocum walked the distance to the bank and tried to calculate where in the maze of tunnels they had to bore upward. He hadn't been too far off, he decided. And Vinson had been right about the rock in this area. It was hard and it would take one hell of an effort to get through. Even if they started working now, they might not be able to get into the bank by Friday night.

Slocum cursed their bad luck. Wainwright would be in the bank on Saturday, and that left only Sunday for the actual robbery. In spite of his intention to be out of the bank with the money two days early, fate had dealt them a different hand.

"Wainwright," Slocum muttered, "what is it about you that I don't like?" Shaking his head, he went off to tell Marla of the problem he and her brother had encountered.

9

"I don't know why you have to go now, John," Marla said, stretching like a lithe cat on the bed. She lay there naked and inviting, but Slocum had other things on his mind. Maybe something more important than Marla Vinson. And his name was Tulley.

"I've got to get to work with your brother soon in the tunnel," Slocum said, dreading going back into the dark, low-roofed mine shaft. Having to slide his feet so he wouldn't stumble in the dark, the constant fear of being crushed, and the tight, cramped, suffocating feeling he got when inside hardly balanced the gain they'd all receive when they broke into the bank vault.

"But Emmett said he didn't want to start until tonight. There'd be carousing and no one would hear if you decided to blast. He's got the black powder, you know."

"He told me," Slocum said. He wasn't sure they could blast their way through the plug of hard rock, but they'd have to find out soon. The weekend was coming fast. Tomorrow was San Jacinto Day and the real crowd would be filtering in all day long from the railroad construction a few miles outside town. By tomorrow night Slocum wanted to be inside the bank and in possession of the payroll.

"You're thinking about something else. Ever since we met up, you've been looking over your shoulder. Who's after you, John? Is it that bounty hunter you mentioned?" Marla sat up in bed, her breasts gently swaying. It made concentrating hard for him. It made lying even harder.

"There's nobody after me that I know of," he said. He bent and kissed her quickly and evaded her grasping hands. Marla would have pulled him back down to the bed for another round of lovemaking. She was insatiable. He just wished he had the time to see if he could eventually tire her out.

"Don't go," she pleaded.

"I'll be back before sundown. If Emmett comes by, tell him I'll meet him at the mouth of the mine."

Slocum started out the door. Marla said, "I hope you stop him, John, whoever he is."

He saw the sad smile on her lips. He said nothing and quickly left before he spilled his guts to her. Putting anything across on Marla Vinson was damned hard. She had seen through him. Slocum didn't think he had showed that much worry about the bounty hunter, but he might have. He had seen men like Tulley before. They got a hair up their ass and just never stopped until they caught their man or were dead.

He had seen the mountainous hulk of the bounty hunter in the Lucky Dice Saloon, so he decided to return and see if the indolent barkeep remembered Tulley. Slocum came in through a side door to check the people inside. He didn't want to blunder into the huge bounty hunter and have to shoot his way clear. The less attention he attracted, the better off he and the Vinsons were.

The casino was going full tilt now, with the railroad men betting what they had saved up from their last monthly pay.

Slocum saw that the railroad bosses were right. Give these men their pay today, and they'd have it spent before midnight. He grinned at this charity on the part of the railroad's management.

It would make him and Marla and Emmett considerably richer.

"What'll it be, mister?" the barkeep asked. He was more active now than he had been the prior day. He had to work to keep the glasses filled. When the parade started Friday morning, the saloon would be shoulder-to-shoulder with railroad construction crews.

By Saturday, the entire town would be overflowing with ranchers and cowboys coming in from their lonely work to blow off a little steam. Slocum didn't intend to join in the festivities—here.

"Shot of whiskey," Slocum said, "and a man who loaned me some money a while back."

"The whiskey's the easy part." The barkeep was already thinking ahead two or three customers, deciding which ones he could give watered whiskey to and which ones would demand full strength. His decisions would mean the difference between a tidy profit and a huge one.

"Big fellow," Slocum said. "Name's Tulley. I got five dollars to repay. Borrowed it from him yesterday right here in this saloon."

"Big fellow?" The barkeep knew who Slocum meant. There had to be a dollar or two to grease the memories.

"Bad-smelling son of a bitch," Slocum supplied. He dropped two greenbacks on the bar. "Wears an uncured hide shirt. No way he could have been polite, but he's got a heart of gold underneath it all."

"Yeah, he was here. Was asking after a guy who sounded a mite like you, come to think on it. I told him there wasn't anyone here answering to your description and sent him on out to the railroad site. There're drifters out there all the time."

"Thanks."

"Wait a minute. If you borrowed money from him and he was here earlier asking for you, that means he was looking for you."

"Right. He knew I wanted something from him." Slocum tapped the two singles on the bar and left before the barkeep could come up with any more questions. The man scratched his head and made the two bills vanish with the pass of his hand.

Slocum had what he'd come for. He knew the bounty hunter had headed toward the railhead. In the hot sunlight Slocum stood and wiped sweat from his forehead. It was a hard ride out to the construction site and back, but he thought the trip would be worth it. He touched the ebony-handled Colt in its holster and knew he would finish off the bounty hunter this time, one way or the other. He mounted up and left Grandville.

It wouldn't be easy. Tulley was like an elemental force of nature. Slocum might as well be trying to lasso a twister. And the ride out and back would be a killer in this heat, but his roan was rested, and Slocum was determined.

The sun beat down mercilessly on his head, but Slocum kept riding. He reached the railroad site a little before two in the afternoon. The site had just about closed down to let the workers go into Grandville for the San Jacinto festivities.

Slocum circled the camp and studied the layout to be sure he knew where everything was. A large freight train had brought new supplies of rail and crossties and had been turned on a temporary circular platform. It wouldn't be long before it headed back the way it came.

Several men clustered around the engine, talking with the engineer. The oiler made his rounds, squirting oil from the long-necked oilcan onto the rods. Slocum knew they were railroad employees and that the solitary man at the rear of the train wasn't.

Tulley looked big even at this distance.

Slocum hooked one leg across the saddle pommel and thought hard. A plan slowly formed. It all depended on how long it would be until the train pulled out on its way back to the supply depot. Slocum guessed the train had come at least a hundred miles. This part of Texas had few towns and they were far apart. A hundred miles meant a good five hours of train time, maybe more depending on the quality of the track that had been laid.

"Five out, five back, and then into Grandville," he muttered. The more he thought, the more he liked what was boiling up in his head. He swung his long leg back over the pommel and found the stirrup. After untying the lariat that rested on the left side of his saddle, Slocum was ready to take on the bounty hunter.

Slocum circled the camp and came up from the far side, using a shallow arroyo for cover. He wasn't able to get as close as he would have liked, but it didn't matter. Tulley spotted him and let out a roar of triumph.

Wheeling his horse around sharply, Slocum put his heels into the animal's sides. He galloped until he came to a small rise hardly more than a sand dune, then slowed and circled, doubling back in an attempt to get behind the bounty hunter. Tulley's horse struggled to run under his rider's massive bulk. The man cruelly whipped the animal to narrow the distance between him and his quarry.

Slocum watched, wondering what sort of man mistreated animals so badly. Treat a horse right, and it might save your life. Abuse it, and it'd die under you and leave you in the middle of nowhere. Tulley wasn't going too much farther on that horse without killing it.

"Be doing a good deed for that poor animal," Slocum said, patting his roan on the neck.

Tulley charged up the rise and slowed. He came to a complete halt and stood in the stirrups, looking for Slocum.

"Where are you, you sniveling coward?" roared Tulley. "You can run, but you'll never get away from me. I swear it!"

Slocum estimated the endurance of Tulley's mount and then let out a long, loud whistle that caught the bounty hunter's attention. Slocum didn't wait around. He put his spurs to the roan's sides and raced back in the direction of the railroad site. The quick trip he had made up the arroyo had shown him the perfect spot for his ambush.

He reached the wash quickly and dismounted, letting his roan keep on for several yards. Slocum shook out his lariat and got a loop ready. It wouldn't be long before the bounty hunter came charging back down the hill, hell-bent for leather.

Slocum waited longer than he'd thought. Tulley was mad, but his horse was nearly dead under him. Tulley cursed and whipped the poor animal until bloody streaks appeared on its flanks. Any sympathy Slocum might have had for the man vanished when he saw how he was beating the horse.

Tulley came racing by the creosote bush where Slocum crouched. As the bounty hunter came abreast, Slocum stepped out, swung the rope in a big loop, and threw it, just as if he was roping a stray. Tulley felt the rope coming down around his shoulders and tried to dodge away, but the forward speed of his horse was too much.

The rope tightened and yanked the bounty hunter from his saddle. He crashed to the ground.

Slocum had taken the precaution of fastening the other end of the lariat around the base of the creosote bush. When Tulley struggled to his feet and tried to run, the tied end fetched him up short. He crashed to the sandy arroyo bottom again. This time he did more than gasp for breath. He stared up into the muzzle of Slocum's six-shooter.

"I don't rightly know why you're so hot to arrest me," Slocum said, "But this is the end of it."

"Like hell!" raged the bounty hunter.

Slocum had been prepared for a fight, but Tulley still took him by surprise. Instead of trying to stand, the man kicked out. A heavy boot struck Slocum just under the knee. His left leg buckled painfully under him. As he stumbled, the pistol left its deadly sighting between Tulley's pig eyes. This momentary lapse was all it took for the bounty hunter to surge to his feet.

"I'm gonna rip your head off," Tulley promised. He lumbered forward, murder in his eye.

Slocum didn't have time to aim at the thundering man. He swung, hoping the barrel would hit something important. He felt the heavy steel crush into Tulley's face. The man recoiled and roared in pain.

"You busted it again. You busted my goddamn nose again!"

Slocum danced away, rubbing his injured leg. It hurt like a son of a bitch, but he was still able to walk. He'd have a prize bruise on his shin, but he couldn't let that slow him now. If he fell into the circle of Tulley's arms, the man would crush him in a bear hug.

"I could plug you where you stand," Slocum said. He didn't know why he didn't simply squeeze the trigger. He had the range. The bounty hunter would be buzzard bait in seconds. But he held off. Tulley didn't seem to be armed, except for his prodigious strength and monumental vitality.

"Pipsqueak," growled Tulley. He wiped away the blood from his gushing nose and started after Slocum again. The bounty hunter didn't seem to fear death and that might have been what kept Slocum from killing him. Six shots at this range would have stopped anything smaller than a grizzly bear. Tulley was big and strong but not that big and strong.

Slocum began circling, pretending his leg was hurt worse than it was. He wanted to lure Tulley into an attack. He didn't have to resort to such subterfuge. The huge man spat blood and then leaped like a pouncing, mountain lion.

He couldn't have played into Slocum's hands better than this. As he came forward, Tulley got his feet tangled in the rope used to lasso him. Slocum grabbed the end and yanked with all his strength. He lost his balance but he also upended Tulley. The bounty hunter landed flat on his back. The loud whoosh told Slocum the bounty hunter had lost all the air in his lungs. Tulley struggled to regain his breath in tortured gasps.

Slocum didn't let him. He stood, gauged the distance, and then dropped knees first onto the man's chest. What air had seeped back into Tulley's abused lungs gusted out again. This time Slocum didn't waste any time. He was good at hog-tying and did a special job on the huge bounty hunter. Three good turns of rope around Tulley's ankles and another circling his wrists had him bundled up and ready for what Slocum had planned.

Catching Tulley's horse was harder than Slocum had anticipated, but he couldn't blame the poor animal for shying away. It had been beaten within an inch of its life. Slocum looped his lariat around the saddle horn and started the horse off at a brisk trot. Tulley was dragged along behind, banging and bouncing off rocks and prickly pear cactus as he went.

When the horse got to the caboose of the train, Slocum caught up and stopped it. He looked around. The engineer was making motions to the crew that the train was getting ready to pull out.

Slocum heaved the unconscious Tulley into an empty freight car and jumped in. It took him another five minutes to get the man trussed up and securely tied to the stanchions inside the car. Satisfied with his handiwork, Slocum jumped back to the ground and slammed the freight car's heavy wood door. He had barely finished his chore when the train's steel wheels began slipping and sliding on the rails. Sparks flew and cinders came from the smokestack. In less than a minute the train had worked up enough power to get moving. In five minutes it was out of sight.

"What you looking at, mister?" asked one of the construction workers.

"The train. Where's it going?"

"We got a depot over in Wichita Falls," came the answer. "A fair distance off."

"Better'n six hours. That's why we need Grandville as a terminus. From there we can go north and west. Nothing much to the south or southwest to interest us."

Slocum smiled and saw the last trace of smoke from the engine vanish in the late afternoon heat.

"You looking for a job? You got to see the construction supervisor."

"Just thinking about a ride on your train when it gets finished," Slocum said. "Good day to you."

He turned his strawberry roan back toward Grandville and left the railroad man staring at him, wondering what the hell the conversation had been about.

10

"I was wondering if you were ever going to show up," Emmett Vinson said. "Leaving me to do all the work isn't like you, John." Vinson stood and brushed off his trousers. He had stacked their equipment just inside the mouth of the mine. Slocum saw four kegs of black powder and enough of the black miner's fuse to let them get a good ten minutes' head start before the powder detonated.

"I prefer dynamite," Slocum said. "It blows up rather than burns like powder, if you don't have it tamped in right."

"I agree," said Vinson, heaving a keg of powder to his shoulder, "but this can be stuffed into crevices better. We might not have to drill all the way like we would to get a good hole for dynamite."

Slocum didn't agree but wasn't in any position to argue.

"What kept you? Marla told me you were on your way, but I expected you a couple hours back. We've lost a considerable amount of time in the tunnel."

"We'll do just fine," Slocum assured Emmett. "I had some business to take care of."

"Business? Marla said somebody was on your trail."

"It's all finished," Slocum said in a tone cold enough to let

89

Vinson know that the matter wasn't going to be talked about any more. He grabbed an armful of shovels and picks and followed his partner into the mine. Before he had gone ten paces he was bent double and imagining the roof collapsing on him.

Slocum went along, trying not to let his imagination run wild. He kept thinking of the money they'd get out of the bank and of Marla Vinson. Emmett had to know what was going on between his sister and Slocum, but he didn't seem to care. Slocum wondered if Vinson even approved in a way. He liked Vinson and Vinson liked him. Was that enough to let common morality ride when it came to Marla?

Slocum hoped that it was. He didn't want the woman to get in the way of either his friendship with her brother or the robbery.

"I've already moved some of the equipment deeper into the mine," Vinson went on, ignoring the coldness in Slocum's answer. "The drill and bit are in place. I thought I might try using it by myself but it takes two men."

"We can do it," Slocum said. He ducked when a particularly low piece of beam appeared in front of him. He wanted this done with. He wanted the drilling to be finished and, if they had to blast, he wanted to be out of the tunnels.

They finally reached the spot where Vinson had originally marked the large chalk *X*. Slocum again counted his footsteps away from the hole where he had stuck the piece of baling wire and found the spot that must be directly under the bank.

"It's only Thursday," Slocum said. "Reckon we ought to try working on it a mite?"

"We won't get through this plug of rock in one night," Vinson said. "We might have to work all night and through part of the day tomorrow."

"That's too risky," Slocum decided. "We've got to get

everyone out of the bank before we dig. What if we break through and the bank's still open?"

"That's a good point," Vinson said. He sat and scratched his chin. "The same can be said about blasting now. If we get too close to breaking through, people might notice."

Slocum had to laugh. Everyone would notice if a huge cavity opened up in the middle of the bank lobby.

"Let's get a feel for what we're up against," Slocum said. He hefted the drill and settled it into a heavy leather harness. Motioning for Vinson to start the rotary, he began driving the steel bit against the rock. After ten minutes he had made only a slight dent in the hard rock. It was as tough as Vinson had claimed. Slocum wasn't sure they could blast through it without bringing the entire roof down on their heads.

"Won't do us much good if we can't use the tunnel after the explosion," Vinson said. "How deep do you think we need to go to get a good upward blast?"

"Deeper than we can dig with this lousy drill. Get the hammer and bits. We're going to have to pound our holes into the rock to get deep enough."

Vinson groaned. This was work, more work than he had intended. Unless they wanted to call off the robbery, though, they didn't have any choice. They took turns holding the heavy steel spike against the roof while the other swung upward with a sledgehammer. In less than twenty minutes they were both winded.

"We're not making much progress, are we?" Vinson observed. "We haven't gone deeper'n my finger." He thrust his index finger into the hole to illustrate his point. "We're going to have to work a whale of a long time to get enough holes for the powder."

Slocum had been sitting and thinking about other ways of getting into the bank from below. Nothing came to him other than more hard work.

"This had better be worth it, Emmett," he said. "I can drive spikes on the railroad and get paid better than I'm likely to on this job."

"The payroll, John, and the bank money from up north. It's all just sittin' in that fat banker's damned vault. And it'll be ours, all ours, when we get in. We've got the combination, remember. This is the hard part."

"We might not make it tonight," Slocum said. "Or tomorrow night."

"Then we'll hit the bank Saturday."

"Wainwright's likely to be working then. This is going according to your original plan, it looks," said Slocum. He didn't like that. It didn't give them enough time to get out of Grandville before Bergstrom opened his vault on Monday morning.

There was another consideration he didn't mention to Vinson. By Sunday, Tulley could have made it back to Grandville.

"Just a little blast, John. That'll be all it'll take to see if we dug the holes right."

Slocum didn't want to go along with Vinson's suggestion. The holes in the rock weren't deep enough. They had worked almost all night. Above, in the streets of Grandville, it was almost dawn Friday. The San Jacinto parade would be starting in a few hours and the people would be out to have a good time. To set off the explosion now might give their entire robbery scheme away.

"We need to do it. We need to know how much more work there is to go before we break through. It's the only way to tell if we get to the vault tonight or have to wait until Sunday," Vinson pressed.

"All right," Slocum reluctantly agreed. He ached and was about ready to drop from the hard work he'd put in all night long. Getting a real job almost seemed preferable to having to spend another night hammering steel spikes into the impossibly hard plug of rock between them and the bank's lobby.

"All we need to do is tamp in enough black powder to shatter the rock sideways," Vinson said. "I was a powder monkey in a gold mine up in South Dakota. Never knew that about me, did you?"

Slocum knew something about placing charges, too, and he wasn't happy with the slipshod way Vinson put the black powder into the holes. He left tiny pockets of air rather than tamping the powder in hard. This would cause many small explosions rather than the one big one needed to bring down the rock.

What worried him the most was bringing down too much of the rock. He didn't want to be standing in the tunnel looking up into Bergstrom's office or his guard's double-barreled shotgun. Not only would the work they'd done be for naught, they'd be in jail waiting to be sent up to the Detroit Penitentiary for bank robbery.

"Push it in harder, Emmett," Slocum said. "You don't want any gaps in the powder."

"I'm doing it right. Trust me, John. You need to be in charge of everything, don't you?"

Slocum flared angrily, though he knew they were both dog-tired and at the end of their tempers from exhaustion.

"Do it right or don't do it at all," he snapped.

Emmett Vinson sat down and wiped the grime from his face. The sputtering carbide light was about dry. They needed more water for it if they were going to spend any more time in the mine. Everything seemed to conspire to hurry them.

"Go on," Slocum said. "Set the fuses and let's see what happens."

"Thank you, John. I appreciate it." Vinson understood what was going on between them, too. He thrust the fuses into the fingers of powder and ran the waxy black miner's fuse away from the area. "I reckon fifteen feet will give us plenty of time to get out of the tunnel."

Fifteen feet, fifteen minutes. Slocum nodded. He was past being able to talk. He would agree to anything just to have this over with.

"There it is. Let's light the fuse." Vinson thrust one end of the fuse into the blazing carbide bit. For a second Slocum thought the fuse wasn't any good; then it sizzled and popped and began burning slowly toward the rock.

"Fire in the hole!" yelled Vinson. "Let's get the hell out of here or it might be our grave."

Slocum gathered their tools and followed Vinson out of the tunnel. He was about fifty feet from the mouth and saw the first light of day showing when the ground buckled under them. Slocum struggled to keep his feet but couldn't do it. He was thrown flat on his belly.

And from the bowels of the mine belched huge clouds of dust and debris.

"Damn, must have put too much in," Vinson said, getting to his hands and knees and shaking off the dirt like a dog getting rid of water. "Didn't think I had, though."

"Emmett, what's that?" demanded Slocum. "Do you hear it?"

"Hear what?"

They were fifty feet from safety and it looked like a mile to Slocum. The shaft was still protesting the blast. Rotted timbers sagged and more dust was pouring down. The entire mine shaft was collapsing and they weren't outside!

"Run, Emmett, run for your life. We got to make it to daylight or we'll be trapped in here!"

Slocum followed his own advice, but he knew it was too

late. Larger and larger rocks pelted down on him from above. Just a few feet from safety a large rock crashed into the side of his head and drove him to the mine's floor. Then the entire roof came crashing down on him, burying him alive.

11

Blackness. Everywhere was suffocating blackness. It took Slocum a few seconds to realize that he wasn't dead. He couldn't be. The dust choked him and the weight on his back was incredible, but he felt and struggled and knew he wasn't dead.

Wiggling from side to side dislodged the largest of the rocks stacked on top of him. He kicked a bit more and got free. He thought he was blind for a moment, then tears cleaned out the grime from his eyes. He blinked hard and wiped at the corners of his eyes until he saw the mouth of the mine shaft.

The day shone bright and hot and promised no rain whatsoever. And that was all right with Slocum.

"John?" came the weak cry. "You there? You make it?"

"Over here, Emmett," he said. Slocum coughed and spat grit from his mouth. "I don't think anything got broke."

"Me, neither," Emmett Vinson said. The two of them struggled to get out of the mine shaft. They both looked as if they had taken jobs as chimney sweeps, but they were unharmed.

"Damnation, the whole mine fell in," complained Vinson.

"Look at that, will you? The whole damn mine fell in. It'll take us all weekend to get it cleared out."

"We might never be able to get it cleaned up enough," Slocum said. He hated to admit that their robbery might be at an end, but the bitter truth faced them. The rotted timbers hadn't been a good sign. Vinson had used too much powder and had brought the entire length down.

"We can do it," Vinson said. "We've got to! I want that money! And it's going to be mine, damn it, it's going to be mine."

Slocum found his horse and drank most of the water he had in the canteen. The dirty taste hardly bothered him. He was alive, and that was what counted most. For a few seconds in there he hadn't thought he'd be worried about drinking or anything else.

"We can do it."

"Emmett, there's no way."

"Not in this tunnel, maybe, but there are others that lead back to the same spot. I mapped them all out."

"Why do you think they didn't collapse along with this one?"

"I'm not giving up," Emmett Vinson said firmly.

Slocum rested for a spell, then heaved himself to his feet and looked over Vinson's shoulder. The man unrolled a large map of the tunnels. Slocum hadn't realized Vinson had spent so much time exploring the underground maze of abandoned mines. A dirty finger marked another path to the spot under the bank. Vinson stabbed down hard and said, "There. There's where we go."

"Give it a rest, Emmett. We're both too tired to do anything now."

Vinson said nothing. He got to his feet, grabbed pick and shovel, and started off. Slocum shuddered. He didn't cotton much to going back underground, especially now that the ill-conceived explosion had weakened even the stronger timbers holding up the roof. But he wasn't going to let his friend go into those mines alone. That was the surest way of dying he knew.

Slocum wasn't certain if he followed Emmett out of friendship or the fear of telling his sister that Emmett had died in a rock fall.

"See, John, you were being too pessimistic. I do declare, you've changed in the past few years. See how it worked out?"

"All I see is a weekend's work ahead, Emmett. That's a heavy rock fall." The roof had collapsed near the spot where they had tried blowing out the rock plug. Digging through to it would take at least two days of backbreaking labor. Even if they got through, there wasn't any guarantee that they'd be able to work their way up and into the bank's lobby.

"I've got to try, John. There's no other way."

"Before you start digging, let's go back to town and see if we blew the floor out of the bank. If we did, we should just ride on out and not look back."

Vinson stopped and considered. "That's good advice, John. There's no way we could pull this off if they knew we were coming."

Slocum trudged back to the mine opening, following the new path they had taken through the labyrinth of tunnels. As before, he rejoiced when the hot sun burned at his face. Just having the option of dying of thirst gave him perverse pleasure.

"The parade's going to start in about an hour," Vinson said. "That ought to cover us well when we poke around the bank."

Slocum wished he had the chance to clean up first. He and

Vinson looked like something the cat had dragged in. Worse, he felt about half past dead. His muscles ached horribly and his back was bruised and scratched from the falling rock in the mine shaft. He wanted nothing more than a hot bath and a sleep lasting a month or two, preferably with Marla Vinson in bed with him.

"We can look now," Slocum said. "There's nobody around there. That's a good sign. If the whole damned lobby floor had fallen in, folks would be poking around to see what happened."

"I heard tell of sinkholes in marshy places. Big holes that open up and swallow entire towns," Vinson said. "There's not much chance they'd think this was a sinkhole, is there?"

Slocum laughed humorlessly. As dry as it had been, the notion of a marshy sinkhole was about as funny a joke as he'd heard in a while.

"There's no one around the bank. Let's just take a look inside."

Slocum and Vinson crossed the street and avoided several drunk cowboys carrying a large banner. Slocum tried to read it but couldn't. The cowboys had tried writing something about Sam Houston on it and had misspelled everything. Slocum wasn't even sure if they could write, but no one seemed to care. They were boisterous and enjoying the celebration already.

"There's nobody inside," Vinson said, rubbing a spot on the plate glass window clean. "I don't even see Wainwright."

"To hell with Wainwright," Slocum said, wanting to forget the teller. "What's the floor look like?"

"I can't make it out. Wait, yes, there! It's all there. Not so much as a sag in it."

Slocum wasn't sure if this was a sign for rejoicing. The plug of rock might be just as thick as ever. The wave of explosion might have gone laterally rather than up through the shaft. The only way they could tell was to shovel through the debris that had fallen in the mine. There might still be long days of work ahead of them.

"Even if we take all weekend to get through, that's fine, John, really," Vinson said excitedly. "The casinos will be pumping thousands of dollars into Bergstrom's vault. Look at the business they're doing right now. Wait till everyone gets in from out of town. Grandville will be the center of the universe then!"

Slocum didn't share his friend's enthusiasm. Most robberies developed trouble somewhere along the way. That was the nature of men having a lot of money and wanting to keep it and other men wanting to take it away. But the Grandville Bank was looking like a harder and harder nut to crack.

"Let's see what Marla's found out," Slocum said. "If we can get through into the lobby tonight, we want her watching from the hotel room down the street."

"This is going to be a great robbery, John. I feel it in my bones."

Slocum walked along in silence. They reached the boardinghouse at the edge of town. He wondered how they could ever get past the landlady. She had an eagle eye and missed very little. She would demand to know what he and Vinson had been up to if they showed up on her doorstep this dirty. Luck held for them. Marla was just leaving. She saw them and motioned them toward the stable out back.

This suited Slocum just fine. He could rinse his clothing out in the stock water and try to feel halfway human again.

"What happened to you two?" asked Marla. She saw the exhaustion on their faces.

Slocum let Vinson explain all that had gone wrong in the mine.

"So you won't be sure you can get into the bank tonight? Damnation," she said, stamping her foot. "That's not all that's bothering me," she added.

"Horace Wainwright?" guessed Slocum.

"He didn't show up for work this morning. Two other tellers did, but not Wainwright. I've been looking around town for him, but he's nowhere to be found."

"Think he's hightailed it out of Grandville?" Slocum asked.

"That hardly seems likely," Emmett Vinson said. "He's more rabbit than man, but he's not going to run like this. He's got a job that pays and security, as long as he puts up with Bergstrom's abuse."

"He could jinx the robbery," Slocum said. "What if he spilled the beans to Bergstrom?"

"He wouldn't do that," said Marla. "He's afraid of his own shadow. I haven't talked to him much, but I've watched him. That day in the bank when we opened the account he was about as nervous as a long-tailed cat in a rocking chair factory. He wouldn't have the gumption to tell Bergstrom. The man would skin him alive."

Slocum had to agree with her on this point. Horace Wainwright wasn't the kind of man to volunteer such information.

"So where is he?"

Vinson laughed. "He might actually have been given the day off to watch the celebration. Bergstrom is a bastard, but maybe he has a spark of patriotism in him somewhere."

"Or maybe Bergstrom thought it was good for business giving his tellers the day off," suggested Marla. "The railroad crew and the ranchers might wonder about a banker who keeps his employees working on San Jacinto Day."

"Keep looking for him," Slocum said. "Emmett and I'll have to get back to the mine as soon as we've rested up a mite. Digging through the debris to get back under the bank is going to be quite a chore."

"All right," Marla said. She turned to her brother and asked, "You do have the combination?"

"Right here," Vinson said, pulling out a scrap of paper. "Wainwright gave it to me the first time we met. I checked on it a couple times since then and he's always given me the same numbers."

Slocum said nothing about Wainwright having the right combination. Marcus Bergstrom didn't trust anyone else with the combination to his heavy vault, after all. Wainwright might have gotten it wrong. But that didn't matter. Slocum knew they had enough powder left to blow the vault door to hell and gone if it came to that. He just hoped that the worst was behind them.

"I'll go to the hotel around seven tonight. It won't be dark until well nigh eight," Marla said. "I've got my pistol, and if anything goes wrong, I'll start shooting."

Slocum wished there was a better way for the woman to give a warning if things turned sour on them. There didn't seem to be any way other than this, though.

"Be careful, you two," Marla said. She lightly kissed her brother's dirty cheek but the kiss she reserved for Slocum was anything but sisterly.

It was enough to make Slocum think everything would work out just fine.

"Four hours we've been digging, Emmett. Is there going to be any end to it?"

"We're close, John. I know it. Look at the maps of the tunnels I sketched. We can't be more'n a few yards away from the damned spot where we blasted."

Slocum wasn't as confident about this as Vinson, but he kept up the backbreaking labor. They had returned to the mine after eating lunch at a small café just off Stoddard Street, in sight of the bank. Throughout the entire meal Slocum had stared at the huge brick building and wondered what was really locked up in its vault. A thousand dollars? Ten thousand? He hardly hoped for that much, though the railroad payroll was likely to be sizable. He had heard that the James Gang had seldom gotten more than a few hundred dollars in any of their daring robberies and that their entire take over years of thievery amounted to less than a thousand.

He and Marla and Emmett might match a lifetime of robbery in a single night. This thought kept him working to move the rock and rubble away from their path through the mine.

"There it is, John. We're just about through. There, there, we've done it! We've done it, John!"

Slocum looked up to see what excited Vinson so much. He aimed his carbide light through the small hole Vinson had dug at the top of the mound of rubble. Then he became as excited as his friend. They were through, and a miracle had occurred. The black powder had brought down sections of roof throughout the mine, making their return difficult, but the powder had also done its work on the rocky plug.

"Not more than a few feet left, John. Look at it. I can taste the money now."

Slocum had to agree. Their goal was just a few feet away. He hadn't thought it was possible that Lady Luck would smile on them this way, but she had. They'd be into the bank on Friday and have two entire days to make their getaway. People would be celebrating in Grandville and would keep the sheriff's office busy with their drunk and disorderly behavior. The deputies would be all tuckered out come Monday morning and would not be inclined to hit the trail looking for bank robbers.

Slocum grinned more broadly. Even if the sheriff had some notion what direction they'd taken, it would be a fool's hunt. There wasn't any way in hell he could catch up with them if they had a two-day head start on a posse.

"Let's not stand around lollygagging. Let's dig!" Emmett Vinson began swinging his heavy sledgehammer with a vengeance. Slocum watched for a few seconds to be sure the energetic activity wasn't going to bring the rest of the rock crashing down, then he joined in.

There were only two feet of rock between them and the heavy wood lobby floor. In less than an hour they had banged away a hole large enough to expose wood planking.

In less than five minutes after that Slocum had pried up the flooring and stuck his head into the bank.

"We're here, Emmett. We made it!"

For the first time, Slocum tasted victory, really tasted it. He swung up into the lobby and the gave Emmett a hand. They had a vault to open and money to carry out.

12

Slocum sat cross-legged on the bank floor for several seconds, not believing they had made it. The crazy blasting, the maze of tunnels, the entire scheme had sounded too farfetched to work this way. He stretched his aching arms and knew the muscles tired out from all the digging would be fine. All it would take was spending the loot they were going to take from the vault.

"The celebration's in full swing outside," Vinson said in a whisper. Louder, he said, "We ought to get the money and go join them. We could buy drinks for the whole damned town."

"We get the money and clear out," Slocum said. This had worked according to his timetable. For that he was glad. Waiting until the last minute made it too hard to escape. Now they could be out of Texas before the banker knew anything was amiss.

And Slocum didn't have to worry about sticking around the town and finding himself face-to-face with the bounty hunter again. Tulley was only a memory now.

"Let's hope Horace had the combination right," Vinson said. He jumped the low wood railing separating the lobby from the bank officers' area. He went back to the heavy vault door and rested his hand against it, as if taking its heart beat.

"We can blow it if we have to. With all the hoopla outside, they'd never hear an explosion," Slocum said. He didn't want to do it that way. This was simpler and less work. And there was a risk of someone hearing the explosion. It would take both of the remaining kegs of powder to pull this monster door off its hinges, but Slocum was willing to do it. The money waiting behind that door seemed to call to him.

"It's almost too easy, John. Everything fell into place so easily. Damnation, I do declare that this might be the finest moment of my life." Vinson's hand shook with emotion.

"Try the combination," Slocum urged. "The sooner we get in, the sooner we can start counting the money."

"True, very true. Let's see now. Three spins to the left, stop at eighty-four, spin back twice—" Vinson set to work on the lock. He cursed when it didn't open the first time. Slocum started to drop back down into the mine shaft and fetch the powder, but Vinson stopped him.

"I might have gotten it wrong," Vinson said. "I'm so nervous my hands are shaking."

Emmett Vinson tried again. From across the bank lobby Slocum heard the tumblers click into place. Vinson let out a choked sound of glee and turned the vault handle. The door opened on silent hinges. Inside rested a big stack of heavy canvas bags.

"Is that all money?" Slocum asked, staring over Vinson's shoulder. "There's ten, twelve bags. Even if there're just singles in each one, Emmett, we hit the mother lode!"

"We did that, John, we did that." Vinson tore open the top bag and pulled out a handful of greenbacks. The bills slid through his fingers and dropped onto the floor. Slocum swooped down like a vulture and grabbed the bills, stuffing them back into the bag.

"Waste not, want not," he said, a broad smile on his lips. Plans raced through his mind: Marla and him, traveling to wherever they wanted. Maybe New York City. He had heard stories about it. Or Boston. A woman like Marla might enjoy Boston. Or, why bother going back East? St. Louis was a fine city. So were New Orleans and Denver. Slocum had always had a soft spot in his heart for Denver. It was a rough, boisterous, growing town that appealed mightily to him. With this kind of money for a stake, he could give General Palmer one hell of a poker game.

"I can't believe we hit it so big, John. Look at this. I'd thought there would be money here, but this much? Never in my wildest dreams. Old man Bergstrom must have been squirreling away every single dime for a dozen years."

"Dimes," Slocum said, worrying about something but not being able to put his finger on it. "Where's the change? A bank this size must use hundreds of pounds of change in a month's time. I don't see any coins anywhere. And there's no bullion. Isn't a bank supposed to have gold, too?"

"Forget the coins. Forget about hauling off gold bars. My back hurts from digging so much. Take the greenbacks!" Vinson heaved a sack of money to Slocum. The weight almost staggered him. And there were eleven others waiting to be stolen!

Slocum took the bag to the hole in the floor and dropped it. Vinson and he formed a kind of bucket brigade to get the money out of the vault and into the hole. As the next to the last bag dropped down, Slocum spun around, his hand flashing toward his six-shooter.

A shot had sounded out in the street.

"Don't go gettin' spooked, John. It's just one of the liquored up cowhands lettin' off steam," Vinson said.

A second shot sounded and a third and a fourth. Two more followed quickly. Slocum ran to the window and peered out into the street. It was as he feared. Marla was leaning out the hotel window. She held a smoking pistol in her hand. He saw her struggling to open the cylinder and knock out the brass to reload.

For a spell he couldn't understand what it was that had made the woman fire. Then he saw shadows moving along the street. The center of the street was lit from both sides where the saloon doors opened and spilled out their inner illumination from gaslights. But the streets were empty of revelers. Everyone had gone inside—except for the fleeting shadows he saw.

"The sheriff's got the place surrounded," Slocum said. "Marla gave us a warning."

"Damnation, how'd they come to suspect?" asked Vinson. He dragged the last money bag to the hole and dropped it down. "Or is it they were just out patrolling and she got spooked?"

"Marla, spooked?" Slocum scoffed at that notion. Marla wasn't the type who frightened easily. Whatever she had seen, she had taken to mean they were in deep trouble.

"You got a point," Vinson said. "That's the last of the bags. Let's get the hell out of here."

Just as he spoke, a bullet ripped through the bank, sending a cascade of glass over him. He ducked and then spun and dived headfirst down the hole they'd cut in the floor.

Slocum was slower to respond. He duck walked to the window and chanced a look into the street, just to be sure. He frowned. He saw four distinct shapes out there but no more. He knew Marla wasn't the nervous kind, but this might be a cowboy who'd had too much to drink whooping it up with a few random shots.

Then he caught the glint of light off a badge. One of the

shadows was a lawman. He had no reason to believe the others closing in on the bank weren't deputies, too.

"Finally decided to join me, eh?" said Vinson. He had hitched six of the money bags into a harness so that, mulelike, he could drag them along the mine tunnel.

"Let me get the flooring back into place. That might make them wonder where we went," Slocum said. He heard more bullets winging their leaden paths through the bank. He tried to figure out what had gone wrong and couldn't. They had been in the bank only a few minutes and had been as quiet as church mice. They hadn't done anything to alert a passing deputy.

He shrugged it off. Sometimes Lady Luck just decided they'd been too lucky and called in a marker. Blowing the rock plug the way they had was lucky. Having the law find them this quickly wasn't. It all evened out. Slocum just hoped they could get away without being seen. He didn't want a posse after him as well as a bounty hunter.

"Tulley," he muttered. Could the bounty hunter be responsible? Slocum doubted it. The smelly bounty hunter hadn't even known Slocum's exact whereabouts when they had tangled at the railroad construction site.

"What's that, John?"

"Never mind. Just keep pulling." Slocum made a harness of his own for the remaining half-dozen bags, but he didn't get too far. He stopped and began laying several feet of black miner's fuse to run to the unused powder kegs.

"What are you doing?"

"Just making sure we can get out of here without a posse breathing down our necks," Slocum answered. He heard the tromp of boots on the floor above his head. It wouldn't be long before someone noticed the hollow sound under their feet and started looking more closely. By then he'd have the tunnel sealed off to prevent any pursuit.

He heard a muffled voice and saw light past a loose plank as someone stepped on it. Slocum lit the fuse and began pulling on the heavy money bags for all he was worth. A second explosion in these old tunnels might bring down the entire maze. If the lawmen in the bank didn't discover the hole in the floor for another five minutes, Slocum knew he and Emmett would get away scot-free.

As he lugged the heavy bags along, his mind turned to other things. He was going to argue with Vinson about cutting Wainwright out entirely. He knew Vinson had said the mousy teller was only doing this for revenge against his boss, but Slocum knew better. Wainwright was the kind of lily-livered coward who would try to blackmail them.

"Backshooter," he grumbled. He had seen the kind before and had recognized it instantly in Horace Wainwright. They never did their own dirty work; they always let someone else do it for them. Wainwright didn't have the balls to stand up to Marcus Bergstrom. He needed Vinson and Slocum to get his revenge for years of being browbeaten. All Wainwright had needed to do was stand up to Bergstrom. If he'd been fired, he would have been better off.

"What's that, John?" Vinson called back. "Didn't hear you."

"Nothing," he said as he dragged the bags. Something else was bothering him, and he couldn't quite put his finger on it. There was something wrong about the deputies being in the street outside the bank. They ought to have been making the rounds of the saloons to keep the peace, not stalking an empty street.

An empty street. A street devoid of drunken cowboys and rail workers who ought to have been celebrating.

"We've been had, Emmett," Slocum called out. "There's something fishy about this entire deal. We've been had, and I don't know how."

"That's a laugh," Vinson said. "How can we be had when—" The explosion from behind sent a cloud of choking dust billowing past. The shock wave drove Slocum to his knees, but he managed to cover his face with his bandanna to keep from gagging. He swiped the patterned cloth across his nose and eyes and got rid of the grime. He found he had to breathe through the rag to get enough air.

"There," Vinson said, recovering. "Does that make you feel any better? We got away clean. There's no way they could have followed us, not with tons of rock blocking the way."

"There's something wrong. I feel it in my bones."

"You have gotten to be an old woman, John. I do declare. You're always coming up with problems where none exist. The only dark cloud on my horizon is not believing we'd get away with this much money. The horses are going to be bowlegged by the time we ride out."

Slocum looked back and saw that splinters of crossbeam had cut through the heavy canvas money bags. And what he saw turned him cold inside.

"Emmett, open your bags."

"What? Not now. We got to—" He clamped his mouth shut when he saw that the carbide light from Slocum's lamp showed a bag half ripped open and spilling its contents.

"There's nothing but cut newspaper in this bag," Slocum said. He jerked out the bag's contents and threw it across the mine. Only a few greenbacks stuffed into the top of the bag were legitimate. The rest was dross.

"This can't be happening," Vinson said, panic in his voice. He tore into his own bags, using the thick-bladed knife Slocum passed him. In the dozen bags they had less than two hundred dollars, all in singles, crammed into the tops. The cursory examination they had given the money bags in the vault showed the money. If they had dug deeper, they would have saved themselves the effort of hauling the bags all the way through the tunnels.

"I don't understand," Vinson said, almost whining. "Wainwright. It's got to be Wainwright. He double-crossed us!"

Before Slocum could answer, they heard the whinnying of horses outside the mine.

"Get the money," Slocum ordered. "Take the real stuff and leave the rest. It's no good to us."

"We got a ton of useless paper," moaned Vinson. "Somebody's gonna pay for this. I swear it. Somebody's gonna pay big for dupin' me like this!"

Slocum rushed to the mouth of the mine and looked out. His heart froze in his chest. There had been four deputies back in the bank. They were cut off from pursuit by the explosion he had set off. But the sheriff and a half-dozen men rode around, checking the openings in the worthless mines.

They would have been neatly trapped between two sets of armed lawmen if he hadn't set off the blast. As it was, they were trapped inside the mine, unable to backtrack because of the collapse in the tunnel.

"We got bad problems, Emmett," Slocum said.

"I'll say. We didn't get more than two hundred dollars. I was counting as I stuffed it into—" Vinson's voice trailed off when he heard the horses' hoofbeats.

"A posse," Slocum said.

"This can't be. The plan. It was perfect."

"They got us dead to rights. There's no way we're going to get away with that many men looking for us," said Slocum.

Even as he spoke the hue and cry went up. A deputy had spotted their tethered horses. It would be only a matter of minutes before they were captured.

13

"I've got the money, John. Let's ride like we mean it," cried Emmett Vinson. He dashed from the mine clutching the small bundle of greenbacks and made for his horse. Slocum tried to judge the distance between them and the posse and their chances for getting away. It didn't look very good. Even considering their horses were rested and the posse's might be tired out from the ride out of town, the lawmen's horses weren't going to be that tired. It was only a few miles from these old mines into Grandville.

"North, Emmett. Go north and we'll try to meet in Kansas City in a month. The usual place," Slocum called. He didn't want to go into too much detail with the sheriff within hearing distance. Vinson would know where he meant.

"What about Marla?"

"We'll have to get in touch with her when we can. We got more important things to do right now, like saving our own necks from the noose."

Someone in the posse let out a howl of glee when he saw Slocum and Vinson making their break for freedom.

The sheriff's men were already galloping full tilt for the two outlaws. The mile or so distance would vanish quickly. Slocum knew they couldn't stand and fight it out, either. There were too many in the posse.

"Good luck, John," called Vinson. "I've got a bad feeling we're both going to need more than that to get away tonight." He put his heels to his horse's flanks and exploded into the night.

Slocum turned at an angle to Vinson and rode off at a somewhat slower pace. He wanted to see if the posse followed Vinson, took after him, or split into sections to get both men. If they went after Vinson, Slocum intended to circle and get back into Grandville to find Marla to tell her what had happened.

He didn't have that kind of luck. The sheriff saw them go down different trails and sent four of his men after Vinson. He led the rest of his deputies after Slocum. The best Slocum could tell, he had five men after him.

There weren't many trackers better than Slocum, or many who knew all the tricks of losing a posse, but Slocum lacked the time to prepare and the flat, dusty land provided no cover. Going was hard on the sunbaked land and the roan was already beginning to struggle. It needed more than the few hours of rest it had gotten while Slocum and Vinson were robbing the Grandville Bank.

Slocum wished for a bright moon to light the landscape. If he kept the roan moving at this speed, it might step in a prairie dog hole and break a leg. Losing the horse would be bad, but being on foot with the sheriff so close would be even worse. He gritted his teeth as he kept the horse moving. He needed moonlight, but he might as well have asked for his own personal lounge car on the railroad going out to the Pacific. Whatever he got this night was going to be from his own efforts and not from wishful thinking.

Looking for a way out didn't help Slocum much. He couldn't see how he was going to elude the posse with them closing in on him minute by minute. A stand of cottonwoods appeared to his left. He veered toward them, wondering if he could use them as cover. He doubted the posse would just ride on by, but he had to try something. Outrunning his pursuers wasn't going to work.

A bullet came whining through the night. It wasn't even close, but Slocum knew the man doing the shooting must have thought he was in range. This gave Slocum even more reason to reach the stand of trees. He hit the ground running, clawing for his Winchester as his boots felt the ground. Slocum stumbled and almost fell. He got his balance and came around, a round going into the rifle's chamber.

The sheriff saw what was happening and called to his men to circle. Slocum cursed his bad luck. He could shoot it out with the lawmen, but the outcome was written in stone. He wasn't going to escape. If he killed any of the deputies in the shootout, he was likely to swing for it. Getting caught for bank robbery was bad enough, but he wasn't likely to be hanged on the spot.

Slocum desperately sought some way out of his fix. He didn't see any way of escaping.

"Give it up, mister. We got you cut off in all directions," the sheriff called. "You ain't gonna make it."

Slocum hated it when a sheriff was right.

"What if I do surrender? What then?" he yelled.

"We won't gun you down. You got my promise on that. We just want the money taken from the bank."

"If I give you the money, would you let me go?"

Slocum knew this was a shot in the dark. It didn't surprise him much when the sheriff laughed at the deal.

"We got you dead to rights. Give up, and we'll see that you get a fair trial. Put up a fight, and you're likely to end up six feet under in the potter's field."

The situation was hopeless. Slocum was on the point of giving up when he heard a commotion. He perked up when he saw a man bent low over a horse and riding like all the demons of hell were on his tail. The posse was taken by surprise and didn't react fast enough to keep the rider from breaking through the ring they had formed around Slocum's refuge.

"Mount up, John. We can make it. There's not enough of them. We can make it!" cried Emmett Vinson. He waved wildly as he raced past Slocum. "There's a way out if we've got the guts enough to give it a try!"

Slocum was willing to do anything to avoid being captured, even believe Vinson had some scheme he had not considered. Slocum swung into the roan's saddle, his rifle still in his left hand.

"What happened?" Slocum put his heels into the roan's heaving sides and got it running. "How'd you get away from the posse after you?"

"Decoyed 'em. Slicker'n snot, it was. There's only six out there on your ass," Vinson said.

"Six?" Slocum cursed. He had misjudged the number. That wasn't like him to make that kind of mistake, but he hadn't been able to get a good look at the posse.

"Don't try to go left or right. They'll get us for sure if we try that. Ride straight down the gully," Vinson ordered. "We'll have to shoot our way out past two of the deputies, but we can make it, John. I know it."

Slocum was in no position to argue. He had to believe Vinson. The man had already evaded four deputies. What were six more?

They galloped along the ravine. Suddenly, appearing on either side, were riders. Vinson shot at the deputy on the right. Slocum took the one on the left. Neither of them came close to winging their targets, but that didn't matter. The sudden gunfire and the foot-long flames from their rifle muzzles spooked the horses. The deputies found themselves fighting to keep in the saddle. This gave Slocum and Vinson the chance to race past.

"We can't stay in the arroyo much longer," Slocum called to his friend. "The sandy bottom's making the going too hard. The horses are tiring fast."

"They weren't in the best of shape when we started," Vinson said. "But we don't have much farther to go. We'll be out of this ravine and can lose the posse in a series of hills."

"Hills? In this country? Are you daft?" Slocum thought of West Texas as flat.

"Not much in the way of hills, I do admit. Certainly nothing as purty as the Flint Hills up in Kansas." Vinson laughed at his little joke. Slocum began to worry for the first time since Vinson had come riding up. If he stood up in his stirrups, he could look over the Flint Hills. They were that flat.

"Where are we going now?" Slocum asked as they came to a halt at the end of the ravine. The high banks had slipped into the gentle roll of the land and there was nothing to give them cover as far as the eye could see.

"But—" Vinson sputtered. He had made a mistake.

"We got to keep moving, Emmett. They'll be on us like a roadrunner on a rattler."

Slocum glanced over his shoulder and saw men on both banks of the ravine. They weren't that far behind. He saw the flashes from their rifles before he heard the reports. And then he heard the whine of bullets cutting through the night. It was getting mighty hot in the middle of the plains.

"We need a Comanche or two to help us," Vinson said. "I'm sorry, John. I thought we could get away comin' out here. I don't know what happened."

"Don't apologize, just ride. We might just stand a chance of outrunning them." Even as Slocum spoke, he knew he was wrong about that. There wasn't any way in hell they could get away from the Grandville sheriff's posse.

And they didn't. Less than an hour later the lawmen had them surrounded on a small rise and took them into custody without another shot being fired.

14

"They got us dead to rights, John," Emmett Vinson said as he rode back to Grandville beside Slocum. "There ought to have been better work on my part. I'm sorry."

"Not your fault," Slocum said. He had plenty of time to consider all that had turned to shit. The bank vault had opened just as Wainwright had said, but the bags stuffed with cut paper hadn't been what they'd been expecting to find. They had been double-crossed, and it had to be Horace Wainwright's doing. That was the only explanation for everything that had gone wrong.

"Hey, Sheriff," Slocum called out. "Was there a reward paid for turning us in?"

"Reward?" The sheriff looked around, startled. "How could there have been a reward offered when we didn't know you were going to rob the bank?"

"You didn't? Then why did you have deputies in the street around the bank?"

"We had a tip the bank would be knocked off tonight. But we expected you to get in the usual way. You know, through the front doors—or at least, through town."

"You can't tell me you were just going for a midnight ride outside town and just happened to come across us," said Vinson. "The mine openings are a ways off your usual patrol area."

"Hardly ever been out there, except when I was lookin' for a little kid who got lost a spell back," the sheriff said. He scratched his stubbly chin. "That's another stroke of luck for me, I'd say. Just when we thought you got away clean, that explosion went off under the bank. Seems somebody remembered that there were old mine tunnels running all over the caprock. That's when I got my men in the saddle and went to look."

Slocum didn't buy that, not entirely. The sheriff had homed in on the tunnel he and Vinson had used like a buzzard coming down on a piece of carrion. There were dozens of the mine openings out in the countryside. That the sheriff had picked the one where they had done most of their work was too big a coincidence for Slocum to swallow. And he knew the sheriff hadn't tracked them there, either. Slocum had been very careful about destroying all trace of their path. Even an Apache tracker would have been hard-pressed to find the trail from Grandville to that particular mine opening.

"Yeah, you surely were lucky this night and we weren't," Vinson said glumly. He shot Slocum a sidelong look. He had a sly smile on his lips that told Slocum he expected to be rescued by Marla.

Slocum looked at the woman as their ace in the hole, too. If they could escape without her aid, so much the better, but he didn't see how they could possibly get away from the posse. They were too attentive, and the ropes fixed around his and Vinson's necks made sure they didn't try anything stupid. Neither of them could ride more than a few feet before the loops would tighten and pull them from their saddles, especially since the sheriff had seen fit to tie their hands behind their backs. Just staying in the saddle was enough of a chore.

"The circuit judge will be making his rounds to Grandville in about a week. We'll have you up on trial then so you don't have to wait too long to know your sentence," the sheriff said. "From things he's said in the past, Judge Warfield's not likely to go easy on you. He hates bank robbers 'bout as much as he does killers."

"Has the judge lost a few dollars in a robbery?" suggested Vinson. Slocum wished his friend would just shut up and let them ride in silence. He didn't care to know of the judge's prejudices or likely sentences. They'd find those out soon enough.

"That's just what happened. He was wiped clean out a few years back and had to start from scratch. He vowed to never let it happen to anyone else." The sheriff chuckled. "Fact is, I was the one what brought them other varmints to justice, too. The judge is likely to see this as a repeat."

"We can give the mo—" Vinson shut up when Slocum kicked him hard. Vinson turned and scowled. He had started to tell the sheriff they could give the money back as partial restitution. Since no one had lost a dime, that had to make the crime seem less in the judge's eyes. But Slocum knew better. If the judge was on a tear, then there wasn't any pleading under the sun that would sway him.

They were looking at a long, long time in prison.

He heaved a deep sigh and settled down to think hard. The more he considered ways of escaping, the more he hoped that Marla kept her head. She was about their only chance to ever see the clear blue sky stretching from horizon to horizon again.

They rode into Grandville just about sunup. Slocum was almost glad to be taken into the jail. He had been unable to keep the rising sun out of his eyes with his hands tied behind his back.

"Into the cell, gents," the sheriff said. "We'll see to gettin' you some breakfast later on. We got to go fetch the banker and talk to him about the robbery."

"Give our best to Mr. Bergstrom," called Vinson.

"Shut up, Emmett," Slocum said. "It's not going to do any good goading them like that."

"The hell you say, John. It does me good." Vinson dropped down on the single bunk in the cell and drew his legs up under his chin. "We got to get out of here, you know."

Slocum was already making a survey of the cell to find its weak spots. The small room was more of a cage, iron bars on all six sides. He dropped to the floor to check, and sure enough, the dirt on the floor just covered bars. He rattled the door and the lock was secure. The hinges would take more than dynamite to blow off and the overhead was completely barred.

"What about the window?" asked Vinson, still sitting on the bunk. "Any chance there?"

Slocum had hoped there would be nothing but mortar holding the bars into the wall. All sides were made from iron bar. The window was just the part of the cage that hadn't been bricked over. Tying a rope around the bars and trying to yank them out wouldn't do anything more than frustrate the horse doing the pulling. They were sealed in for good.

"The only way is through the door. Where do they keep the keys?" Slocum asked.

"In a small drawer in the sheriff's desk," Vinson said. "I don't think there's any way of reaching it from here."

"Then Marla's got to be the one who gets us out. We can't grab a guard and get out that way, not if the keys are still in the desk drawer."

"You think the sheriff would swap one of his deputies for letting us go free?"

Slocum shook his head. If they did manage to overpower a guard, he wasn't sure the sheriff would let them make such a swap. The man seemed good-natured enough, but there was an iron core to him that Slocum hadn't missed. The lawman looked to be one tough customer when push came to shove.

"There might be another way," Slocum said.

Before he could tell Vinson what he had in mind, the sheriff returned with Marcus Bergstrom and Horace Wainwright. The three men sat in the outer office. Slocum and Vinson could see them through the open door into the room.

Slocum motioned Vinson to silence. He wanted to hear what was going on, and he wanted to be sure he was right in blaming Wainwright for them being caught so easily.

"It's a credit to my employees," Marcus Bergstrom was saying, "that they were thwarted in the act. I have to commend Mr. Wainwright for his cleverness and devotion to duty that he reported to me immediately."

Something in the way Bergstrom spoke put Slocum on guard. The banker was too sarcastic. He was goading Wainwright. The banker might have been trying to make Wainwright confess to more, but Slocum wasn't sure. What seemed to be a lead pipe cinch was that Wainwright had chickened out at the last minute and had notified the sheriff about the robbery.

"Wasn't that the way it was, Mr. Wainwright?"

"Please, Mr. Bergstrom. Don't make me tell it again."

"Horace has a confession to make, Sheriff. Go on, Horace, tell him what really happened." Bergstrom sounded cocksure of himself now, completely satisfied that he was driving the nail into the coffin of the man who had betrayed him.

What the teller said infuriated Slocum.

"I did have a part in the robbery, Sheriff," Horace Wainwright said at Bergstrom's insistence. "But not too much. They offered me so much money for the combination to the vault that I couldn't refuse."

"Horace has fallen on hard times. He was too proud a man to come to me with his problems, however," Bergstrom said. Slocum knew a lie when he heard it. If Wainwright had problems, Bergstrom would have laughed at them or maybe even foreclosed on his teller's house, just for a bit of amusement.

"He allowed their silver devils' tongues to entice him to reveal the combination to the vault. Isn't that true, Horace?"

"Yes, sir." Wainwright was staring at the rough wood flooring and looking the world like a young schoolboy caught cheating on a test.

"But he repented. He told me about it, and I had him contact you, Sheriff." Bergstrom frowned. "Poor Horace didn't know the full details of their plan, however. That's why it came as something of a surprise that they didn't ride into town and break into the bank in the way we had thought most likely." Bergstrom was puffed up with himself. Slocum wanted to grab his thick-jowled neck and squeeze the life from him. The look he shot Slocum from the outer office was enough to make Slocum mad enough to bend the iron bars of the cage.

"That explains why there wasn't anything but cut paper in the bags," Vinson said softly. He rattled the bars in his frustration. "That son of a bitch wanted to slow us down and let us break our backs lugging off the bogus money bags."

"We caught 'em fair and square, Mr. Bergstrom," the sheriff said. "They put up a little fight, but we were too much for them. The deputies did a good job of circlin' and roundin' them up."

"Glad to hear it, Sheriff. You've done a marvelous job. I trust that you will see fit not to deal too harshly with Mr. Wainwright. He did confess before the crime had been committed."

"Well, sir, I don't rightly see that any charges need to be brought. We got the pair what done the robbery. If anything, you might consider Horace's problem to be more of moral weakness than mortal sin."

"I won't do it again. I know what happened, sir. If you give me another chance, you won't be sorry."

"I'll give him another chance," grumbled Slocum. "I'll even give him a five-minute head start."

"You're a more generous man than I," said Vinson. "I want his ears to hang on my belt, the backstabbing son of a bitch."

Slocum didn't respond to that. He hadn't trusted Wainwright from the instant he'd laid eyes on him. The weak-chinned kind were always trouble, and Horace Wainwright was no exception. He didn't even have the gumption to come clean with his boss—and it had been Bergstrom he had wanted to screw out of the money.

"No," said the sheriff, "there's no need to bring charges. I think Horace has suffered enough."

"I have, sir, I truly have." For the first time Wainwright looked up. Tears glistened in the corners of his eyes.

"There will be a reward for the capture, of course," Bergstrom said. "You and your deputies did a fine job, considering the problems with the rowdies from the railroad and the ranches."

"There's no call for that, Mr. Bergstrom. I do need some information about the robbery, though. You mentioned the railroad crews. You said there was a payroll in the bank vault?"

"There was, Sheriff, and there was a special shipment of money from the federal bank in Kansas City to give loans to the poor, drought-stricken ranchers. I had not yet had time to properly allocate that money."

"So what are we lookin' at in terms of money, Mr. Bergstrom? We recovered well nigh two hundred dollars."

Bergstrom let out an explosive sound that startled Slocum and Vinson. They leaned hard into the bars in their cage to see what had provoked the banker.

"Two hundred! Sir, there was damned near eighteen thousand in that vault. I thought you had caught them red-handed!"

"We did," said the sheriff. The man frowned and then scratched his stubbled chin. "You sayin' there's still seventeen thousand, uh, eight hundred dollars missing?"

Emmett Vinson rattled the bars and shouted, "You lying sack of shit! There wasn't anything in that safe but cut paper!"

Marcus Bergstrom turned and looked back at Slocum and Vinson. The feral gleam in his eyes told the entire story. The banker said, "That's exactly what I mean, Sheriff. You haven't come close to recovering the full amount taken."

For the first time, Slocum realized just what a predicament he and Vinson were in. When Wainwright confessed his part in the robbery plans, Bergstrom had turned the theft to his own benefit. Bergstrom would waltz off with damned near eighteen thousand dollars and pin the entire robbery on the two men in the cell.

Slocum sat on the single bunk and shook his head. They had planned a perfect robbery, but it was Marcus Bergstrom who had profited.

15

"That miserable son of a bitch," grumbled Vinson. He sat on the dusty jail floor, his head resting on his knees. "That incredible thievin' son of a bitch! I do declare, if I get out of here, I'll wring his fat neck for him. I'm so mad I don't know whether to spit or go blind."

Slocum let his friend continue to grouse. He was busy pacing the iron cage, checking what he had already checked, seeing if there might not be some small flaw in the bars, the floor, the ceiling, the walls, the door. The more he studied the situation, the more certain he was that getting out of this cell would require more ingenuity than any ordinary jail. Whoever had constructed the Grandville jail had done a first-rate job of it and had given the citizens their money's worth.

"Marla," Vinson said suddenly. "She's the one who's got to spring us. There's no other way out. They've got us caught like wolves in a lockjaw trap."

"We don't want her involved," Slocum said a mite too sharply. Vinson looked up and stared at him.

"I know you're sweet on her, John, but we're looking at one hell of a long time in prison if she doesn't do something to spring us from this hole. That crooked banker's the one who stole the money. You know what we got."

"It was all fake money," Slocum answered absently. His mind was turning over a plan to get them out. It was daring, but it required even more courage to stay in the cell and face the judge in a week. From all the sheriff had said about Judge Warfield, he was as likely to tell the sheriff to throw the key away as he was to give them a fair hearing.

With people in town and out on the railroad site up in arms over having their money stolen, Slocum wasn't sure if being in the cell wasn't the safest place for them. Bergstrom had done them a foul turn and he had done it perfectly. He could walk away with the money—and Slocum wasn't sure if it was even close to eighteen thousand—and point the accusing finger elsewhere.

Horace Wainwright. Marcus Bergstrom. Slocum wasn't sure which man was more worthless. Wainwright didn't have much of a backbone, and Bergstrom's greed was more than any two men ought to put up with.

"It's partly our fault," Slocum said suddenly.

"What? What's our fault?"

"Greed. We plowed into that vault and never once took the time to think about what was missing."

"You going on about the coins again?" Vinson shook his head and pulled his knees up a bit further. He looked like a man already on his way to the gallows.

"Coins, specie, there wasn't any metal in the vault. Bergstrom can't run a bank without gold in some form. We ought to have known that, but we were too blinded by the bags of money to think. All we wanted was to get out of there and start spending."

"He snared us good, I'll say that. But how are we going to contact Marla? She's got to get us out of here. The longer we stay, the more likely some law-abidin' citizen's going to be to suggest we get strung up for our dirty deed."

"You're too dependent on your sister, Emmett," said Slocum. "There might be a way out of here, but it'll take some doing. Are you up to it?"

"I want out real bad."

Slocum nodded. He wanted out, too, and it wasn't just a matter of freedom. Nobody crossed him the way the banker had and lived to brag about it. There were many kinds of justice in the world. Slocum's kind was all that was likely to hold Bergstrom to account for what he had done.

"Can you figure a way of putting out that gaslight over in the corner?"

"Reckon I can," Vinson said. "When do you want it out?" The gaslight hissed and popped as it burned. The jet needed cleaning and had left heavy carbon deposits around the small sconce under it.

"In a spell," Slocum said, stripping the blanket off the bunk. He stuffed it into the window and made as tight a seal there as he could. He fumbled in his pocket and got out a tube of lucifers. He went over his plan in his mind, looking for problems. It was dangerous, and they might end up burned or dead, but he thought it was worth trying. Staying in Grandville for trial was a surefire way of going to prison.

"Dinner's supposed to be comin' sometime soon," Vinson said. "Think that's the time to make our try?"

"It has to be," Slocum said. "The deputy will have the key with him. There might even be two of them, one to stand back a ways as guard and the other to open the cage. It won't matter, if the one with the key gets close enough."

Vinson saw what Slocum planned and made no suggestions. Slocum took that to be a good sign. Emmett was with him all the way on this, even though they might end up in the potter's field outside Grandville.

"Get the light out," Slocum said, studying his pocket watch. He ran his finger over the case and thought of his brother Robert. He had died during Pickett's Charge; the watch was the only legacy he had left. Somehow, touching the case gave Slocum the determination to carry through. His brother had never slacked for an instant. He wouldn't either.

Vinson spent ten minutes working to get the light out. He pulled a plug of tobacco from his shirt pocket and chewed for a few seconds, then spat. The first gob missed the flame by several feet. Vinson kept chewing and spitting, getting closer and closer.

"I'm running out of spit, John. It surely is dry."

"You can always try something else." Slocum checked the watch and worried that it was taking Vinson too long. Before he could say anything, there was a hiss and the light sputtered out. The flame was gone, but the gas jet continued to spew forth its gaseous fuel. Slocum motioned for Vinson to sit on the floor. The air in the room would get close soon with the single window blocked. He hoped that their dinner came before they passed out from lack of air.

"Getting a mite close, John," Vinson said ten minutes later. "Maybe you ought to go on and light one of the lucifers. Might blow the top off the cage."

Slocum shook his head. The iron cage was too secure. He wasn't sure a stick of dynamite would take the door off its hinges, much less destroy enough of the bars to let them squeeze through. The only way they were going to get free of the jail was by the door, after a key had opened its lock.

"All right in there, suppertime," came the gruff voice. The door into the sheriff's office opened. The light beyond showed two men, one holding a tray and the other with a shotgun.

"What'n the bloody hell's going on in there?" demanded the man with the tray. He coughed and dropped the food. He staggered into the room. Slocum saw the key in his hand.

"The gaslight's out. They're being gassed to death," cried the deputy with the shotgun.

"Now, John, do it now," croaked Vinson. He lay flat on his belly, the gas almost overwhelming him. But Slocum held back. He had it all in his head where the two deputies had to be for this to work, and they weren't in place yet.

"Get 'em out 'fore they croak," ordered the second deputy. The one with the key hurried forward, one hand over his nose. The key in his other hand held Slocum's full attention. This was what he had been banking on.

The instant the key was thrust into the lock, he struck a lucifer. The gas ignited and blew the deputy back through the office door and into the other. The rush of flame outward set fire to their clothing and all the papers in the outer office.

And Slocum managed to reach up and twist the key in the lock. The cell door opened and they were free.

"Let's get the hell out of here, John. I don't think I can take much more. I'm woozy and feel like pukin' my guts out."

The fire had spread throughout the wooden portion of the jail. Slocum checked and saw that the deputies were still alive, though singed. He grabbed one of the unconscious men by the collar and dragged him to the door. He motioned for Vinson to get the other deputy.

"They haven't done us any favors," Vinson complained.

"There's no good reason to want them dead," Slocum said. He didn't want to antagonize the sheriff and the townspeople further. Bergstrom had done a good enough job of that. Killing two of the locals might mean a posse that would chase them to the ends of the earth. As it was, he didn't think Bergstrom had made many friends. If the people considered their loss Bergstrom's fault, they might be a tad slower getting together a posse to chase down the bank robbers.

Slocum wasn't counting on it, but he didn't want outraged relatives ready to string him up as soon as they caught him.

"We might not be able to get out of here," Slocum said honestly. "There's still a powerful lot against us."

"Granted, John, but there's more going for us. Here, catch." Vinson had not only pulled the second deputy from the burning jailhouse, he had retrieved their pistols. Slocum strapped on his cross-draw holster and felt the familiar pressure of the Colt Navy on his left hip. It felt damned good.

"Let's not wait around to help with the bucket brigade," he said. They sprinted for the saloon across the street, spun, and put their backs to the wall as the saloon emptied of patrons. The half-drunk customers pointed and shouted and created enough of a ruckus that Slocum actually thought they might get away after all.

The more confusion there was in Grandville, the harder it would be for the sheriff to get his deputies together to track them down.

"To the stables," Slocum said. "That must be where they put our horses."

"Might be better to steal someone's else's horses. That'd keep them guessing for a while longer," suggested Vinson.

"They'll know soon enough we're not in there." Slocum jerked his thumb in the direction of the burning jailhouse. The wooden structure was just about turned to cinders by now. Only the stark black iron cage remained, and he could see that the door was standing open. The sheriff wasn't stupid enough to think they'd been in there when the jail was going up in smoke.

Vinson shrugged. He agreed with Slocum on the need for speed. They ran to the stable at the edge of town and carefully peered inside. The stable hand had left to help fight the fire. In most towns, fire was an enemy that knew no bounds. The Texas drought had added to the danger. If the fire at the jail wasn't stopped, everything in Grandville was likely to end up in flames.

Slocum said, "There are our horses, watered and fed, and there's our tack."

"This is the first real piece of luck we've had," said Vinson, saddling his horse. "Where do we go?"

"How do we get there is a better question. Do we split up and make them chase both of us or do we try to make it together?" Slocum rummaged through the supplies in the stable and found a canteen and some cornbread the stableboy had brought for breakfast. Vinson added a stick of jerky he found in the tack room to the pile and they divvied up their meager supplies for the trip.

"Kansas City still sounds like a good place to end up," Vinson said. "And I know the hotel. I've got some unfinished business there."

"Let's ride out a ways together," said Slocum. "We can see if we've got company on the trail. If we do, we split and make our own way the best we can."

"Fair enough. I've seen enough of Grandville for a lifetime, though I do wish there was some way I could get back at that banker man."

"Later," Slocum said, thinking the same thing. He carried a grudge for a long time, and Marcus Bergstrom had earned one powerful hatred. He'd pay, but the day of justice would be sometime in the future.

Now all Slocum cared about was leaving town a free man.

"The flames have spread," Vinson observed. "I hope Marla returned to the boardinghouse and didn't stay in the hotel. It's too close to the jail for comfort. Already a saloon has caught fire."

Slocum stared at the dancing flames without any hint of remorse. He hadn't wanted to set fire to Grandville, but it had been the only way he could think of to get out of the jail. With any luck, the townspeople would have the fire out soon. By then he would be miles out of town and looking back at the thin column of black smoke rising, the only marker showing where he had almost been convicted of bank robbery.

"Think we ought to pick another direction to travel from the one we chose before?" asked Vinson. "The sheriff might decide to try this way just because we'd gone north when he chased us from the mines."

Slocum considered the notion of going east and then turning north to Kansas City. "Let's do it," he decided. "There's every point on the compass we can run. No point in giving the sheriff a way of cutting down on the possible paths, is there?"

They rode steadily until the first light of dawn. Slocum reined back and found a high point to study the dry land while Vinson gnawed on the stale cornbread and bit off a piece of the beef jerky. He sipped at the water and made a face.

"The water tastes alkaline," he said. "Still better than rolling a rock around to get some spit moving on your tongue, though."

Slocum was barely listening. He found Grandville and saw the smoke rising, just as he had pictured. But there was something wrong. He couldn't pin it down, but he had a gut feeling they were in a world of trouble.

"I don't want to waste too much time, Emmett," he said. "And it might be a good idea if we did split up and went separate ways."

"Is there somebody on our trail already? I do declare, that sheriff is a house a fire!" Vinson laughed at his own joke. He sobered when he saw Slocum wasn't laughing. "What's wrong, John? You got that long face again."

"I don't know what's wrong," Slocum said. "But something is. I just feel it." His cold green eyes worked across the dry West Texas prairie and saw nothing out of the ordinary, but his belly tightened into a cold knot. Trouble was brewing and he didn't know where.

16

"There's no one on our trail, John. You're getting spooked over nothing," Emmett Vinson said. He shielded his eyes as he looked into the east. "Looks good, John, if a mite on the dry side."

Slocum didn't answer, because he saw nothing. He silently went to his roan and mounted, intending to put as much distance between him and the Grandville sheriff as possible.

"You're lettin' your imagination work on you," Vinson went on as if Slocum had answered. "You used to be different, John. Don't know why you're getting so cautious in your old age."

"There's trouble out there," Slocum said. "I want to get out of Texas."

"Not a Ranger," Vinson said. "The bank robbery, even burning down the whole town around their ears like we did, isn't anything to interest a Texas Ranger."

They rode in silence until the noonday sun drove them to find shelter. A leafy cottonwood afforded them enough shade to rest their horses. Slocum lounged back and stared at the cloudless blue sky. The sun had crept up until it was just about at the zenith. He tried to figure out why he had the feeling he was being chased.

"The wicked flee where no man pursueth," said Vinson, as if he had read Slocum's mind. "But we're not all that wicked. Hell, Bergstrom is the real criminal. What we did was an honest day's work. What he did was low-down."

"What we did wasn't honest," snapped Slocum. "Don't try to put a different face on it. But you're right about Bergstrom. He owes us plenty."

"I figure the debt to be well nigh eighteen thousand dollars," said Vinson. "Do you reckon he really had that much in his vault, or was he lying through his teeth?"

Slocum started to answer, but a sound brought him bolt upright. His hand flew to his pistol. He drew and cocked the Colt in a smooth motion before rolling to his side.

"What's the matter?" Vinson looked around, his hand resting on the butt of his six-shooter. Then he heard the tiny sound that had alerted Slocum. He drew, also.

Slocum motioned for his friend to circle to the right. He went left, an ominous feeling in his gut. He carefully made his way around the tree, down a small ravine, and then back, looking for some sign that the posse had managed to sneak up on them. He had watched their trail all day and hadn't seen a telltale cloud of dust rising to mark the passage of even a single horse, but he knew he might have missed some of the signs. The wind had whipped across the plains and could have masked pursuit.

"John! Come on over here and take a look at what I found."

"What is it?" Slocum called back. When Vinson didn't respond, Slocum grew even more cautious. He dropped to his belly and wiggled across the dry land until he got to a spot where he could look down from a small incline. Emmett Vinson just stood under a cottonwood, his arms hanging limply at his sides. He moved back and forth but made no effort to conceal his presence.

Slocum moved closer, and then he saw the rope around his friend's shoulders. Vinson's head hung at an angle and a tiny river of blood trickled from his temple. Someone had roped him, tied him to a tree branch, and then coldcocked him.

"Try anything, Slocum, and I'll cut you into small pieces and feed you to the buzzards."

Slocum knew better than to try any sudden movements. He looked back over his shoulder and saw the bounty hunter standing behind him, a shotgun with a bore larger than any steamboat on the Mississippi River pointed squarely at his back. Tulley could make good on the claim of cutting him to ribbons.

"You led me one hell of a chase. I don't cotton to that. I'm used to runnin' in my quarry and collectin' my due. Slide that fancy-ass gun of yours back into its holster. No! Don't roll over. Get up on your hands and knees and do it."

Slocum did as he was told, seething the entire while. He had been cautious, but not vigilant enough. He had expected a half-dozen men, not just one. And he had never thought he would see Tulley again after he'd dumped him in the railroad car bound for Wichita Falls.

"How long you been back in these parts?" Slocum asked.

"Get that leather thong over the hammer," Tulley said, ignoring the question. Only when Slocum's pistol was secured in its holster did the bounty hunter ease up a mite.

Slocum stood, hands above his head.

"I got you dead to rights, you and that no account partner of yours," Tulley said. "I don't remember him from any of the wanted posters, but that don't matter. If he's ridin' with you, there's a reward on his head. I'll bet money on that fact, yes sir."

Slocum said nothing. Tulley broke into a wide grin. Two of his front teeth were missing. Slocum didn't remember noticing that the last time he'd run afoul of the bounty hunter.

"I chewed my way out of them ropes," Tulley said. "Cost me my two front teeth, but it was worth it. I got off the train less than twenty miles from where you put me on. Took a spell gettin' back, but here I am."

"How'd you find us so fast?" Slocum found it hard to believe that any man could track them like that. He and Vinson had chosen a route at random after they broke out of the Grandville jail.

"Luck started shinin' on ol' Tulley, she did," the bounty hunter said. He waved the huge shotgun in the direction he wanted Slocum to walk. They went down the slope to where Vinson moaned softly. The man's eyes fluttered open. It took him a second to focus on Slocum and when he did, his lips moved in a silent apology.

"That's all right, Emmett. It wasn't your fault. There's no getting away from him," Slocum said.

"Shouldn't have let him make me decoy you like that. But the shotgun. So big." Vinson passed out again. Slocum touched the wound on the side of his friend's head and saw that Tulley had driven the butt of his shotgun into Vinson's skull. It was a nasty wound but nothing that would leave more permanent damage than the memory of a very bad headache.

"I just happened across you," Tulley said. "Luck. Just luck, but I knowed what to do, this time. You're a sneaky one, Slocum. And you're gonna do time—after I get my reward."

"You don't have a warrant for me," Slocum pointed out. He had carefully shredded both the arrest warrant and the two wanted posters.

"Don't make no never mind to me. We'll go back to Grandville and they got a telegraph. I'll get another one.

Maybe find what this one's wanted for and collect the reward on him, too." Tulley poked the unconscious Vinson with the muzzle of his weapon.

Slocum weighed his chances against the huge bounty hunter and knew he had lost any advantage he might have had. Tulley had them both dead to rights.

"Let's just go on to the next town. It's closer than Grandville and they got a telegraph, too. I'm sick of this desolate land and we're running short of water."

"We're goin' back to Grandville," Tulley said firmly. "They got better saloons." That settled the matter. Slocum had hoped to get to another town where the sheriff and the townspeople weren't out for blood because he and Vinson had damned near burned their town to the ground escaping from jail, but it hadn't worked. He resigned himself to the ride back to Grandville.

"This is truly one peculiar place," Tulley muttered to himself as they rode into Grandville. Men with shovels were digging everywhere. The graveyard had a dozen eager excavators making holes hardly larger than their heads, and the shallow holes stretched over the horizon, or so it seemed to Slocum. The entire population of Grandville had turned into demented prairie dogs.

By the time they got to the center of town, Slocum understood. Posters everywhere offered a thousand-dollar reward for the return of the loot from the bank robbery. The men of Grandville thought he and Vinson had buried the money before getting caught and were hunting for it, digging up any place that might have had a spade of earth turned in the past six months.

Slocum saw that Tulley didn't react to the posters. He realized the man couldn't read. But that didn't stop him from being able to match pictures up with their owners. He saw the ones of Vinson and Slocum and a wide smile split his dirty face.

"How much they offerin' for you here, Slocum?"

"Nothing," Slocum lied.

The bounty hunter laughed. "I can read," he said. "They're willin' to give me two hundred dollars for the pair of you."

Slocum knew then that Tulley couldn't read words, but the numbers meant something to him. It irritated Slocum that the bigger reward was being offered for the return of the money, but then that was the way Bergstrom would have done it. The money could never be returned. The crooked banker had it squirreled away somewhere safe. If someone happened to turn up any money from some other source, the banker would be doubly happy. As for the men who had done the robbery, Marcus Bergstrom was probably just as happy if he never saw them again. A trial might bring out unwanted questions he couldn't answer. Slocum snorted in disgust. Horace Wainwright might even decide to tell the complete truth about what had gone on.

"Well, well, what have we here?" came the sheriff's calm voice. "Where'd you find these two owlhoots?"

"Got 'em out east of town, Sheriff," Tulley said. "I brung them in for the reward."

"Mr. Bergstrom will be glad to give it to you, I'm sure." The sheriff paused for a moment, then asked, "What about the money? Did they have it on them?"

"Money?" The bounty hunter didn't know what was going on. "I fetched 'em back so's I could get paid my bounty. This one slipped away from me twice before. Not this time."

It took the sheriff a few seconds to understand what was going on. Then he laughed. "How much is the reward on Slocum?"

"One hundred dollars. And I saw another hundred on this one." Tulley prodded the still unconscious Vinson, who lay across his saddle, hands tied under his horse's belly.

"What was their crime?"

"You ought to know. You got the posters put up," snapped Tulley. "What's wrong with you, Sheriff?"

Slocum cleared his throat and spat grit. "He's trying to do you out of your reward, Tulley. He wants it."

"Shut that filthy mouth of yours," the sheriff snapped. Slocum said nothing more, but saw that the damage had been done. Tulley got defensive and moved his shotgun from one side to the other so he could cover the sheriff.

"It's not like that," the sheriff said. "They burned down our jail and a saloon after they robbed the bank."

"Am I going to get my reward?" Tulley's voice was icy cold in the hot, dry wind whipping down the Texas town's street.

"We'll get it for you."

"Or some of it," Slocum put in just loud enough for Tulley to hear. "The sheriff's got to make a living, too, you know."

Tulley spun and hit Slocum on the side of the head with the long shotgun barrel. The powerful blow knocked him from his saddle. Slocum landed hard in the dusty street and lay there trying to regain his senses. But the pain he had received was worth the seeds of distrust he had sewn between the two men. Tulley wouldn't believe the sheriff now, no matter what happened.

"We can't put them back into the cage. They burned the whole damned thing down and the fire damaged the lock. We'll put them over in the Lucky Dice's storage room out back of the saloon."

Slocum and Vinson were thrown into the dank room. Slocum sat down and took a deep breath. It was almost enough to make him drunk. Whiskey had been stored here recently, which explained why the storage room was like a small prison cell. The saloon owner didn't want anyone breaking in and helping themselves.

"What's going on, John? I don't remember much of the ride into town," Emmett Vinson said. "My belly feels like I been kicked by mules all day long, though."

"You have," Slocum said. He began working on the ropes tying his hands. They came free in a few minutes; then he worked on Vinson's. He explained their predicament and how the bounty hunter had come to be on his trail.

"You should have told me, John. We could have worked that out together."

"How better to get rid of Tulley than tie him up and put him on a fast train for distant parts?" asked Slocum.

"You do have a point. You handled it as good as we could have together without putting the bastard in a shallow grave." Vinson rubbed his hands in the darkness and then said, "So how are we getting out this time?"

This time Slocum knew they'd have to rely on Marla. He had no idea how many men were on guard outside the storage shed, and trying to find out was likely to get their heads blown off, if not by the guards then by the bounty hunter.

17

"It sounds as if Tulley is putting up quite a fight," Slocum said, leaning against the wooden wall of the storage shed that was his prison. He tried to find a knothole, but there wasn't one large enough that let him get a good view of the argument the bounty hunter was having with the sheriff.

"Hope the sheriff blows his damfool head off," grumbled Vinson. "And I do declare, I never smelled a man who stank that bad. Even in a drought, you'd think he could do something about the odor."

"He wears that uncured hide shirt," said Slocum, more intent on eavesdropping than talking to Vinson.

"You know how some of the Indians cure hide? They piss on it after they've chewed it a while. Might be a good thing Tulley didn't try curing that shirt, after all. He could have killed us just with the smell."

Slocum's attention came away from the argument for a moment. He thought how easily Tulley had captured them out on the plains. The bounty hunter had come up from downwind, Slocum recollected now. If he had tried approaching them from any other direction, both the horses and Slocum would have reacted. Slocum wondered if the bounty hunter knew he stank to high heaven or if he just thought it was the way folks smelled naturally.

He turned back to the verbal fight between the bounty hunter and the sheriff.

"I tell you, Sheriff, I ought to get all the money, not just the money for the wanted posters."

"There aren't any wanted posters, Tulley. As far as we're concerned, you get the reward offered for bringin' those two varmints in and not one cent more."

"I'll take 'em back then!" the bounty hunter roared. "I can get more at some honest town."

"They're not leaving my custody," the sheriff said coldly. "They hid eighteen thousand dollars, and there's not a soul in this town who doesn't want to get it back. That represents a goodly portion of the town's life savings."

Slocum snorted at this. They weren't the ones who had stolen the money. It had been Marcus Bergstrom, and he had been robbing the citizens of Grandville blind for years.

"I don't care what else they done," Tulley said petulantly. "I want my due for bringin' that Slocum to justice. He's got warrants out on him all over the place. You just telegraph around and find out."

"Tell me where," the sheriff said tiredly.

"I don't rightly remember where I got those posters," Tulley said. "I picked up an arrest warrant because I showed a poster to a judge over in the Piney Woods country."

"Tell me where," the sheriff repeated, "and I'll see about getting you the reward. Otherwise, you're going to have to settle for the money Mr. Bergstrom offered."

"I want what's due me," Tulley grumbled, "and I'm gonna get it come hell or high water."

Slocum didn't hear the sheriff's response. He wasn't the kind to take any guff off the bounty hunter, no matter how big and intimidating the man was. Slocum leaned back and tried to picture the outside of the shed. Breaking in ought to be harder than breaking out. It was a storage shed designed to keep drunk cowboys away from the kegs of whiskey, not keep dangerous prisoners locked up for long.

"There's no trust between the sheriff and the bounty hunter," Vinson remarked, "but I fail to see how we can turn this to our advantage. Having Tulley break us out is no improvement."

Slocum had to agree. Tulley was likely to leave Emmett and collect the reward on him, then take Slocum to some town where there was a wanted poster hanging in the marshal's office. Not being able to read and not being able to remember where he had found the original wanted posters was working against the bounty hunter. Slocum could thank his lucky stars for this small boon.

"How can we contact Marla?" Slocum asked, thinking aloud. He needed to give her information about the shed, about the best way of springing them from its confines.

"Don't rightly know, John," answered Vinson, thinking his friend was talking to him. "If she had a lick of sense, she'd've left town right after the fire started."

"She's still here," Slocum said. "I feel it."

"I said, if she had a lick of sense. She's a Vinson. That means she's a bit daft in the head, and of course she's still in town. She knows we wouldn't get too far." Vinson lounged back on the dirty floor, his feet propped up on an empty crate. "She knows we didn't get too far because our luck has run dry. I'm never going to make it back to Kansas City."

"What's so all-fired important in Kansas City?" Slocum asked.

"It's nothing, John. Marla's got to be in town. She'll know we're down on our luck. She will. She will!"

Slocum didn't know if Marla's thoughts would run along that course, but he did think she would come for them. When she did, he wanted to be ready. He examined the walls and found them secure. Only then did he climb on a crate and begin checking the roof. It had been nailed down, but in one spot the dry weather had caused the nails to pull free a few inches. Slocum looked out into the alley behind the saloon.

He wished there had been something interesting to see. Try as he might, he couldn't pry the roof up another inch against the long nails used to fasten it. He gave up and began checking the floor, going around on hands and knees.

"Need light," he muttered. "Would help if we had one of those carbide lamps we used in the mine."

"They're not about to give us anything that could burn the place down. It was just luck you had the lucifers back in the jail. Who'd have thought we'd set fire to the place locked up in an iron cage?"

"How much of the town has gaslight?" wondered Slocum. He kept coming back to what the townspeople would fear most: fire. The drought made putting out even a small fire a deadly job.

"Some of it does. I noticed it in a couple of the saloons," said Vinson, "but that's not going to do us any good."

Slocum hated to admit that Vinson was right. Even if Marla was somehow able to set fire to a saloon or another business, that didn't get them out of the shed. As far as Slocum could tell, there was one armed deputy guarding them at all times and there might be more. With Tulley getting as belligerent as he was, the sheriff might decide to assign another man or two to guard duty as well. He looked like a damned fool letting them get away the first time. He wasn't the sort of man who repeated a mistake.

"She's got to do it soon," Slocum said. "The longer we're here, the more likely they are to keep us."

"The more likely they are to lynch us, you mean," said Vinson.

"Who's getting down in the mouth now?" asked Slocum. He settled down, his mind working over all the possible ways out. He saw none. They were fed by a tray shoved through a notch cut in the bottom of the door. The iron locking bar outside was never removed, nor was the heavy padlock, which held it in place.

Mostly, Slocum wished for a window like they'd had in the jail. He wanted to be able to stare out at open spaces and savor the illusion of freedom. Locked up like this in darkness was worse than any punishment they could have meted out.

Slocum dozed off, only to come awake around one in the morning. He heard the guard mumbling something. Slocum pressed his ear against the panel and tried to make out what was going on.

"—can't leave now, honey. The sheriff would skin me alive if he came by and found me missing."

"But there's no other time," came a whiskey-roughened female voice. "I got to go back to work soon. This celebration has the cowboys worked up and hornier than all get out."

"But—"

The guard's tone told Slocum he was weakening. Slocum wondered how he could take advantage of the guard's absence. There didn't seem to be any way he could turn the event into an escape.

But he had to try. He put his hand over Vinson's mouth and woke his friend. In a whisper he told him what was going on outside. Emmett came awake immediately. The pair of them started trying to pry the roof up against the nails. The faint screeching sounded louder than cannonades in the night, but they kept going.

Vinson grabbed Slocum's arm and forced him to stop when they heard the grating of a key in the lock.

"We need something to hit the guard," Vinson whispered hotly. "What are we going to do?"

"We've got fists. Let's use them. Get on the other side of the door," ordered Slocum. "We'll both tackle him at the same time, you low and me high."

They got ready for their attack. The door opened a fraction of an inch and Slocum launched himself. He crashed into the door and slammed it open. His arms closed on the person outside as Vinson followed him out, tackling his victim. They went down in a struggling heap.

"What are you two doing?" came Marla's aggrieved question. "I'm rescuing you, not wrestling you like some crazed grizzly bear."

"Sis!" cried Vinson. He forced himself to his hands and knees. "It surely is good to see you."

"I do declare, you've gone strange in the head, Emmett. And you, John, you're going along for the ride, I see."

Slocum guiltily pried his arms free from around her slender shoulders. She carried their gun belts and weapons. Slocum grabbed his Colt Navy and checked it. All six cylinders were loaded and ready for action.

"I'm not so dumb as to give you an unloaded six-shooter," Marla said in disgust. "But we can't stand here jawing all night long. The guard's going to be back any time. From all Mary Beth says, it never takes him more'n a few minutes."

"Mary Beth?"

"She's a whore in the Lucky Dice who's sweet on the deputy. We got to talking and I offered to fill in for her while she and her beau spent a few minutes together. There'll be hell to pay when she finds out I didn't do any such thing."

"Let's get out of here," Vinson declared. "I've had my fill of Grandville. Which direction do we go this time, John? East, north, or do we try for the border? Mexico's lookin' better and better to me all the time, even if it isn't Kansas City."

"We're not out of here yet. We got Tulley to contend with and the sheriff's not going to let us just ride on out without getting riled." Slocum shut the door and refastened the heavy padlock. Unless someone decided to check, there was nothing to show that they weren't still inside. He hoped that the deputy didn't think to look when he returned.

"Damn, there he is now," said Marla. "Run, John, Emmett, run!"

"Wait!" Slocum saw that the deputy would see them for sure if they tried running. "Get around the shed. Try to sneak off as quiet as you can. I'll be along in a few minutes."

"What are you going to do, John?" Marla's hand clutched at his sleeve.

"Buy us some time. Where are our horses?"

"At the same stable they were before," she answered. "We'll be waiting there. Just don't get caught again."

Slocum touched the ebony handle of his six-shooter. He wouldn't be captured again without some gunplay. If that happened, people would die, and he didn't intend for one of them to be him.

Marla and Emmett Vinson rushed off into the night. Slocum slipped around the shed and waited until the deputy got back into position. Then he banged his hand against the wall and yelled, "I want something to drink. It's damned dry in here!"

"Go to hell," the deputy said, sitting on the ground, his back to the shed. "You'll get water with breakfast. Till then, it's nothing. Me, I don't think you even deserve breakfast, but the sheriff says you got to be kept presentable for the judge."

Slocum made a comment about the judge's ancestry and then added a few choice words about the sheriff's. He subsided and then waited to see what would happen. The snores from the deputy told him he had convinced the man he and

Vinson were still in the shed. This might have bought them precious hours.

He followed Marla and Emmett to the stable, weaving in and out of shadows and avoiding being seen by any of the drunken revelers in the streets. Even if the celebrants had seen him, Slocum wasn't sure they would have been able to identify him. San Jacinto Day had gone well for the saloons. He reached the stable just a few minutes after the other two had arrived. They were mounted and waiting and had already saddled his strawberry roan. He patted the faithful animal's neck and it rubbed its head against his shoulder. Once more the horse had been watered and well fed.

"No food to steal this time, John," said Vinson, "but Marla's thought about that and packed us some fine victuals."

Slocum saw that Marla was saddled and ready to ride, also. He didn't know that it was smart for her to come with them. So far, the sheriff had no idea there was a third member of their gang.

"I'm coming with you," she said firmly. "It doesn't matter if the sheriff finds us together or not. If he does, I'll just say that you kidnapped me. That might get us out of another jam."

"If Tulley comes after us, it won't matter. He's as likely to run the three of us in as he is to shoot us." Slocum worried more about the bounty hunter's persistence than the Grandville sheriff.

"We won't be caught. This time we'll make it," Vinson said. His usual optimism had returned. "We'll be in Kansas City before they even know we're gone. Why, they'll be trying an empty shed and sentencing it to a hundred years in jail!" He rattled on and on with his fantasies about how clever their escape would be.

Slocum rode in silence, acutely aware of Marla's hot eyes on him. He found himself wanting her. He had been through hell and he needed her close to reassure himself that it hadn't been for nothing. This line of thinking turned to a parallel one and this one began to rankle. The more Slocum thought about Marcus Bergstrom, the more he found himself hating the man.

"He's the one responsible for our problems," Slocum finally said.

"What's that? Who are you talking about? That smelly oaf of a bounty hunter?" Vinson and Marla had been quietly talking, letting Slocum brood. They fell silent and waited for him to respond.

"The banker," Slocum said with venom in his tone. "He did this to us. He's the one who stole the money from the bank. If he hadn't cut us out like he did, we'd be rich now and spending the money in style."

"So? We're in hot water now, if this drought leaves enough for them to boil us in," said Vinson. "We're better off hightailing it for parts unknown."

"Bergstrom cheated us, and he's going to get away scot-free with eighteen thousand dollars," Slocum said coldly. "I don't want to let him get away like that. The money's rightfully ours. We stole it fair and square."

"What are you saying, John?" asked Marla.

He didn't answer. The grim set to his body and the cold look in his eyes told her all she needed to know. John Slocum wasn't going to be accused of a crime he hadn't committed. If he was going to be pursued for robbing the Grandville bank, then by damn he was going to be the one who ended up with the loot from the robbery.

If Marcus Bergstrom just happened to catch a bullet along the way, all the better.

18

"This is dangerous, John," said Emmett Vinson. "We can't stick around Grandville too long. Come morning, they'll find we're not in that shed. Then all hell's going to be out for lunch."

"Think of Tulley," urged Marla. "You said he wasn't the kind to give up easily. Nobody's going to pay him for an escaped prisoner, even if it wasn't his fault you and Emmett got away. He's going to be madder'n a wet hen."

"Everything you say is true," Slocum conceded, "but I'm not going to let that fat-ass banker keep our money. We worked hard for it, and I mean to recover it." He remembered his aching back from all the work digging in the mine tunnels, and he remembered almost being buried alive. The fear and hard work had to be rewarded somehow. Eighteen thousand dollars seemed like a damned good way to reward their efforts, Slocum thought.

"What's he going to say, other than we came by?" Vinson said suddenly. "He can't say he had the money. We can take it from him and waltz off with it. They think we've got it, anyway. John's right. We might as well be hanged for wolves as for sheep."

"No," Marla said. "There'll be other banks, other chances. Try to get even with Bergstrom and this will blow up in your faces. He's a mean one, that banker man." The woman looked at Slocum and saw the true significance of mean.

She turned to her brother. "Talk some sense into him, will you, Emmett? This is crazy. You'll never see Kansas City again if you go along with him."

For some reason, this argument held great sway with the man. Emmett Vinson heaved a deep sigh. "I was comin' around to your way of thinking, John, but I do declare, she might be right. This isn't the smartest thing you've ever come up with." He glanced back over his shoulder toward Grandville. "They'll be stirring in a few hours, and then they'll be buzzing like bees. The whole damned town is likely to come after us, and this time I don't think they'll want us to stand trial. Let's forget it and just ride on."

"You and Marla can ride on. I'll catch up with you later." Slocum spoke aloud as the plan formed in his head. He hadn't listened to one thing Vinson had said about this being dangerous. "Maybe Marla can lay a false trail while you take off in a different direction. If they catch her, there's no reason to hold her. You can go to Mexico and I'll shake the money from Bergstrom's tree."

"John, please," the woman pleaded.

"This is a good plan," Slocum said firmly. He didn't want to part with Marla again, but he did want her out of the line of fire. If she rode on, she might draw the attention of the posse that was sure to come after them. Even Tulley wouldn't be inclined to take her back to Grandville. That would mean a delay in finding his two escaped criminals. There wasn't a reward offered for Marla.

"No!"

Slocum looked at the woman. "Use your head. Stick with us and there's a good chance you'll be caught, too."

"We worked that out. I'll just say you kidnapped me, then divert their attention and—"

"Do you think that'd work?" The scorn in Slocum's voice silenced her. "This is a better plan. Lead them on a wild-goose chase, if they even pick up your trail. That gives Emmett a chance to get away and me time to find the money."

"Splitting up would give us a better chance to get away," Vinson said. "And you going a different direction, Marla, increases John's and my chances." He turned to Slocum and said, "I just don't like you tackling the banker alone like this. Where would you start? Bergstrom doesn't look to be the kind of gent who scares easily."

"He's fat but he's tough," Slocum agreed. He already had a few ideas about where to start. "I'll do all right with him. We can meet in a few months. Kansas City?"

"Why not?" said Vinson. "We been promising one another that long enough now. We might as well keep at it."

"If I get the money, we can divvy it up then. If not, you two are free."

"John!" Marla Vinson reached out and touched his cheek. "Don't do it this way. Please, I'm begging you. Let's get away together."

"I want the money from the robbery." His words echoed across the still night and stood on their own, as if carved in stone. Slocum was determined, and not even Marla Vinson was going to stop him.

"Marla, let's do it his way. Come on," Emmett Vinson urged.

She bent over and gave Slocum a quick, unsatisfactory kiss. "There'll be more when we all get to Kansas City," she promised. Then she wheeled her horse around and took off at a pace that was unsustainable for more than a mile. Slocum didn't care about that. He was glad she had made a quick break. If she had stayed for even a few more seconds, he might have relented.

"See you in a month or so, John. And good luck." Vinson reached over and slapped Slocum on the shoulder. Then he rode at right angles to the path taken by his sister. Slocum was left alone on the prairie, under the bright points of the stars, with only his thoughts of revenge to keep him company.

Slocum stayed in a shallow arroyo the entire day, enduring the burning sun and lack of water. He dug in near the roots of a mesquite and found some damp soil. It wasn't much, but it kept him from going crazy with the heat and thirst. He dozed fitfully, never quite willing to sleep because of the possibility of a posse finding him. His nose worked constantly, as much against the dust as to sniff out the bounty hunter's rotting shirt. And when the cold night descended on him, he was bug-bitten and ready to kill.

He made his way into town, carefully watching for any indication that he had been spotted. The San Jacinto Day celebration had wound down. Slocum wondered where the sheriff had put the drunks now that the only cell in town was a stark iron skeleton in the middle of a field of embers. He wasn't about to stop and ask anyone.

His goal was simple. All he wanted to do was find Horace Wainwright. The day had given him time to think, if not clearly then at length about all that had happened to him in Grandville. Marcus Bergstrom was a crooked son of a bitch who had money Slocum wanted. That was simple enough.

Even simpler was the way Wainwright had sold them out. Slocum wasn't interested in the reasons. He probably could come up with a dozen better than any Wainwright would offer. What Slocum wanted was a taste of revenge before moving on to the crooked banker.

He watched the bank carefully as the coal oil lamp inside was extinguished. Bergstrom was too cheap to even use the town's gaslight system. When the mousy teller came out, Slocum was ready. He followed him across town, out past the cemetery, to a clapboard house of modest means. Only when a light came on did Slocum approach, his hand resting on his Colt.

He peered through a side window to be sure Wainwright was alone. The man hadn't spoken of a wife or children in his confession. If there had been any, they would have added credence to his apology. Slocum wasn't surprised to see that Wainwright lived alone.

Still cautious, though, Slocum circled the house and looked in each window of the four rooms. Except for Horace Wainwright, the place was empty. Slocum waited until the night darkened a bit more and Wainwright sat down for his simple supper. Only then did he jiggle the door slightly, get it off its latch, and slip inside.

"Good evening, Horace," he said softly. "It's good to see you again."

The man almost went through the roof in surprise, a forkful of food shooting off and splattering against the far wall. The rabbitlike teller turned absolutely pale when he swung around and faced Slocum.

"You," he choked out.

"I'm glad to see you, too, Horace," said Slocum. He perched on a counter, his six-shooter aimed directly at the teller's face. Slocum knew how imposing this looked. He counted on it to terrify Wainwright.

It worked.

"I didn't want to do it, Mr. Slocum. He made me. He forced me. He's a devil!"

"You mean Marcus Bergstrom?"

"Yes!"

"Now, how did he find out about the robbery in the first place, unless you double-crossed us?"

"I didn't! I swear, I didn't tell him. I hate Bergstrom. He's a fiend. You can't know how awful the man is!"

"I can guess," Slocum said coldly.

"Don't kill me." Wainwright dropped to his knees and looked as if he were praying. "I'll do anything, anything! Just don't kill me."

Slocum almost pulled the trigger. He hated men who groveled. He had never liked Wainwright, and he had always known the teller lacked guts. Telling Emmett Vinson that the teller was the weak point in the robbery hadn't done any good. Wainwright had still betrayed them, and Slocum took that as a personal failing.

But damn it, he hated it when a man groveled like Horace Wainwright was doing now.

"Why not tell me exactly what happened? How did Bergstrom come to know you had given us the combination to the vault?"

"I—he—"

Slocum moved the muzzle of his pistol a mere inch so that Wainwright was no longer staring down it. The teller swallowed hard and started over.

"He came to me and told me he knew everything. I pretended not to know what he was saying. He told me he had seen me with ruffians planning to rob the bank."

Slocum sighed. Bergstrom had probably seen Wainwright and Vinson together. The teller's normal routine didn't include going to saloons and carousing with rough looking drifters. It didn't take much intelligence to guess something unusual was happening. A guess about a bank robbery wasn't too farfetched. Bergstrom had known nothing; he had frightened the truth from his teller. Slocum was even more disgusted with Wainwright than before.

"So you told him when we were going to rob the bank."

"I had to!"

"But you didn't know how we were going to get inside."

"No."

Slocum frowned. The deputies in the street were enough to take care of a pair of bank robbers, but that didn't explain to his satisfaction how the sheriff had known straight out what portion of the mines to ride to after the detonation had brought down the roof on the shaft they had used to escape. It was possible that Bergstrom had done more investigating on his own than was apparent.

"Did Bergstrom know about the tunnels under Grandville?" Slocum asked.

"He must have," Wainwright said. "He loaned money to most of the miners. When none of them paid off, he was the one who foreclosed and shut the mines down."

"Could he have been thinking about getting in and out of his bank the same way we did—through the tunnels?"

The confused look on Wainwright's face told Slocum the teller wasn't privy to the banker's thoughts. Whatever Bergstrom had plotted would be as much a mystery to Wainwright as it would be the rest of the town. Slocum could make a few good suppositions, though. Bergstrom wanted a way in and out of the bank to fake a robbery. When Vinson and Slocum had come along, he had launched a plan that had already been building in his twisted mind. They had played right into his hands.

"What about the money?" Slocum asked, deceptively calm. Inside he seethed with rage at Bergstrom and the mousy teller.

"The money?" From the gobbling tone in Wainwright's voice, he knew exactly what Slocum meant. "I don't know. You took it. You—"

"Bullshit," Slocum said. The pistol came back and centered between Wainwright's wide, frightened eyes. "Bergstrom's got the money. Where's it likely to be hidden? He set us up. He planted fake money bags after robbing his own bank. Where's the money?"

"I don't know! Honest! You got to believe me, Mr. Slocum. I don't know."

Slocum was inclined to believe the teller.

"I'm going to Bergstrom's house and ask the same question. If you don't want your face blown off, you'll stay here and pretend you never saw me. Is that clear?"

"Yes, sir, yes! I wouldn't do anything to cross you."

"Vinson isn't with me. If you try turning me in to the sheriff, he'll find you and skin you alive. Then he might decide to really torture you. How much pain can you take?"

"I won't breathe a word of your visit, sir! Please don't do anything to me." Wainwright started crying. He turned Slocum's stomach.

"Where's Bergstrom's house?"

Slocum got the directions and left. He sat astride his horse for almost ten minutes, waiting and watching Wainwright's house to see if fear was going to hold the man in his place. When he saw no hint of movement, Slocum started for Marcus Bergstrom's.

He had a score to settle with the banker.

19

Slocum took his time getting to Bergstrom's house. He didn't want to rush in bullheaded and find himself surrounded by the sheriff's deputies. He was still close to Grandville and didn't have any idea how the lawmen had responded to the latest jailbreak. An even bigger concern for Slocum was the bounty hunter.

What about Tulley? The man wouldn't get his reward since Slocum and Vinson had escaped. He wasn't likely to take this sitting down. The huge bounty hunter had a temper, and Slocum had seen his skill in tracking. Tulley had sneaked up on him out on the plains, and Slocum had never known he was coming. The bounty hunter had caught Slocum completely unawares.

Slocum studied the slow wheeling of the spring stars overhead. He waited until just after three in morning before getting to Bergstrom's house. He wanted the banker to be sound asleep and all the more startled to have a six-gun shoved into his face. The fright might be enough to pry loose the information about his hiding place for the stolen money. If it wasn't, Slocum wondered if he would be content to just pull the trigger.

The banker's house sat on a small knoll overlooking town. Below him, Slocum saw the occasional gaslight flickering in Grandville. Above, there was nothing but darkness and the looming house. By West Texas standards, it was a mansion—nothing as grand as the Creole mansions in New Orleans or Commodore's Row in St. Paul, but still a cut above the average. Bergstrom lived well.

Now he would catch hell for it.

Slocum started up the winding trail when that sixth sense of his began gnawing away at the back of his mind. He slowed and finally stopped. He strained hard to hear the slightest sound in the still night air. Nothing.

What alerted him was his nose. The scent of sulfur on the wind told him someone had just struck a lucifer. He didn't remember Tulley smoking. And there wasn't the awful stench of his hide shirt carried on the clean night breeze. Just the sulfur and, following it closely, the sharp scent of tobacco.

Someone was smoking, and they were upwind from Slocum. He looked around and found a small clump of creosote bushes at the base of the hill. Tethering his horse, Slocum checked his six-shooter and then started circling. It didn't take him more than five minutes to see the bright glow of a coal at the tip of a hand-rolled cigarette, which betrayed the exact location of both the smoker and his companion.

Dropping to his belly, Slocum moved forward until he got within earshot.

"If he wasn't paying us so much, I'd say to hell with him. Old man Bergstrom foreclosed on my pa. What do owe him?"

"Yeah, he foreclosed on my place last year—damn drought. But he is paying us good to just sit and watch. What do you think's got him so spooked?"

Slocum moved carefully and came out on the hill jus

above the two men. A third slept quietly, wrapped in a blanket. The two standing guard weren't paying much attention to what went on around them. Slocum could have gone up the hill to the house, but he wanted to know more about Bergstrom's sentries.

"Ought to let those cutthroats have 'im," grumbled the second man. "Sure, he pays good, but he can afford it. He already stole most of the land around Grandville. When that railroad gets here, Bergstrom's going to be filthy rich."

"He's rich already. What's he need with more money?" asked the first. He stubbed out his smoke and Slocum lost sight of the men. Only slowly did they become more than shadows moving through shadows.

"There's never enough money." The second man sat on a stump and fell silent. The man who had been smoking hefted a rifle and went on a slow patrol of the area. Slocum trailed him silently, watching and waiting for others. He came across them less than a hundred yards away.

"That you, Joshua?" came the call.

"It's me," came the answer from the man Slocum followed. "Anything?"

"Johnny got spooked by a rabbit leaving its burrow. Other'n that, there ain't been a thing. Not a soul moving tonight. I think Bergstrom's got a hair up his ass on this one."

"So take his money, drink his whiskey, and to hell with him," suggested the man called Joshua. "That's what we're doing."

Slocum made his way farther up the hill, away from the two sentry points. He didn't doubt that there were others posted to keep him and Vinson away from the banker. That they didn't do their job well was no concern of Slocum's. He wanted the money from the bank and as soon as he got it, he would be on his way. It didn't matter if half the town of Grandville stood between him and the eighteen thousand dollars. He was riled and he'd get his due.

He moved like the wind until he got to the south side of Bergstrom's house. Slocum froze when he heard movement above him. He pressed his back against the wall and looked straight up. He saw the toes of boots poking over the eaves of the house. There was at least one sentry on the roof. The toes vanished. Slocum counted himself as lucky. He hadn't heard the man until the last possible instant to hide.

On the front porch sat a man with a rifle across his lap. He looked alert, but Slocum heard soft snoring sounds. Getting past him and through the front door wasn't going to happen. A board would creak and alert the guard. The hinges would squeak, or something would stick and need to be forced. Slocum looked for another way into the house.

Every window was securely nailed shut. Bergstrom wasn't taking any chances. Slocum wondered if the man was roasting to death inside the tightly shuttered house. It was little enough retribution for the woe the banker had caused.

Slocum kept looking for a way in and found it under the house. The building had been constructed on a slight slope. Rather than spend days leveling the area, bricks had been used to build up one corner. Slocum slid under, aware that he might be entering a rattler's den. Considering who lived above, Slocum wasn't sure that he didn't prefer a sidewinder's company.

Wiggling along, Slocum peered up through the floorboards now and again to be sure he knew where he was headed. He found the bedroom without any trouble. A small lamp burned and cast a wan light through a knothole in the boards. Slocum pressed his eye to the knothole and looked around.

Marcus Bergstrom worked on a set of ledgers at a desk. The lamp was shielded on all sides but that toward the banker. This explained why Slocum hadn't seen any light shining out the window. He couldn't be sure, but Bergstrom might have lowered heavy black silk curtains to further cut the possibility of light escaping. The banker toiled in private, not wanting anyone to intrude.

Slocum tested the floor for a loose board. He figured he could rise up and get the drop on the banker before Bergstrom could even look up from his ledgers. Slocum was disappointed when he discovered all the boards were firmly nailed in place. Try as he might, he couldn't budge a single one. He finally gave up and wiggled around to find another room to rise up like Leviathan from the depths, bringing his retribution.

Again he was thwarted. All Slocum got from his subterranean excursion was dirty. Frustrated, he wiggled out from under the house. He looked at the constellations overhead and estimated that he had spent close to ninety minutes getting here and scouting the area. It would be daylight in another couple of hours. As much as he hated doing it, he had to pull back and wait for another chance to confront Bergstrom and get the money. With a small army camped around the house, Slocum didn't want to be trapped here in daylight.

He hesitated before starting down the hill. He might stay under the house and catch Bergstrom. Then Slocum put that crazy idea out of his head. The guards would find his horse tethered at the foot of the hill and come looking for him. And Bergstrom would probably be in town when that happened. He wouldn't get a chance to put a round or two in the fat banker's gut.

Disheartened, Slocum retreated, skirting the two posts of guards he had found on his way up. A gentle breeze from below blew against his dirty face and gave him some solace.

It also carried an unmistakable message. His nose almost clogged when he smelled Tulley.

Slocum went to ground instantly, his hand flashing to his cross-draw holster. He didn't know how far away the bounty hunter was, but he was close. Damned close.

It took only a few seconds before Slocum saw the man working his way up the hill. Slocum didn't know how the bounty hunter had gotten on his trail again, but the man followed it like a bloodhound. Bent almost double, Tulley came uphill like an avalanche in reverse. There didn't seem to be any escape from his implacable advance.

Slocum retraced his steps, thinking the guards might stop the bounty hunter. He got all the way back to Bergstrom's house before he realized that Tulley was at least as good at tracking and avoiding the guards as he was himself. Slocum cursed as he burrowed back under the house. How was he to get away?

He was caught between Tulley and Bergstrom's guards, and he still had no idea where the banker had stashed the money from the robbery.

His Colt came easily to hand. Slocum sighted at the spot where Tulley was most likely to come into view. A single shot would end that problem, but it would start a passel of others. Every guard would come alert and converge. They'd all want to know who had gunned down the bounty hunter, and Bergstrom would want to know how Tulley had come this close to his house without being discovered.

The ensuing search would easily uncover Slocum. It couldn't help but do that, because he had nowhere to hide.

What other choice did Slocum have?

The bold answer came to him just as Tulley slithered over the crest of the hill and started toward the house. Slocum fired three times, missing the bounty hunter each time. Then he started yelling.

"There he is! I plugged the son of a bitch! I got him! There he is!"

Slocum settled down, reloaded his spent rounds, and watched as guards boiled out of hiding like ants from their hill. Tulley squalled like a stuck pig and opened fire with his heavy shotgun. The roar of that prodigious weapon was enough to wake the dead.

In the confusion, Slocum slipped out from under the house and onto the porch. "There he is," he yelled at the man with the rifle. "I think you plugged him dead center. God, what a good shot!"

The confused guard rushed off to see the results of his supposed marksmanship. Slocum hadn't even known the man had fired, but he guessed that he had. From the amount of lead whining through the air, everyone was firing at everyone else. Let Bergstrom's guards eliminate one another. All Slocum wanted from this pandemonium was to be free of Tulley.

Slocum crashed into the heavyset Bergstrom as the man tried to leave his house. The impact caused them both to reel, but Slocum recovered first. He lifted his pistol and aimed it squarely at Bergstrom's face. This had worked well with Horace Wainwright. It would create just as much fear in the banker.

"Good evening," Slocum said. "Where the hell's the money?"

He had counted on shock to loosen the banker's tongue. With Marcus Bergstrom it didn't work. The banker let out an incoherent roar of rage and grabbed a chair, flinging it at Slocum. Slocum fired, but the bullet went wide as Bergstrom ducked his head.

The banker dodged faster than Slocum would have thought possible for a man of his size. And as he rushed from the room, he screamed for his guards. Slocum let off another round to keep Bergstrom moving away from the door. Then he followed cautiously.

He was glad that he did. Bergstrom had found a pistol and opened fire on Slocum. The bullets sailed wide of their target, but Slocum was forced to retreat.

"Slocum!" came the roar from the doorway behind him. "Now I got you, you slippery son of a bitch!"

Tulley came blasting into the house like some elemental, unstoppable force of nature.

Startled, Slocum emptied his pistol at the bounty hunter. He wasn't sure any of the rounds found their target. Tulley bellowed, but Slocum couldn't be sure if it came from the pain of bullets ripping his flesh or the victory of again finding his quarry. Tulley's long arms spread like a dark cloud as he tried to get Slocum in a crushing bear hug. It was Slocum's turn to dodge and duck. He got under the bounty hunter's groping hands and let Tulley go past into the room where Bergstrom was making his stand.

More bullets came from the banker, this time aimed at Tulley. Slocum saw that he couldn't stand and fight. Everyone was after him. Bergstrom might kill Tulley, but there was a small army outside all devoted to preserving Bergstrom's worthless hide. And there just wasn't a chance in hell he could search the house to find the eighteen thousand dollars Bergstrom had stolen from his own bank.

Slocum dived through a window, the glass tearing at his hands and arms. One piece raked his chin, but he landed on the front porch unscratched by anything more than glass. Bullets filled the air around him. He lay still for a moment, waiting to see what happened.

The guards came rushing up, but they were after Tulley, not him. Slocum took the time to reload. Then he got away from the house and went to the small barn out back.

"The damned money," he grumbled to himself. "I want the damned money."

He watched the ebb and flow of battle and heard the constant gunfire, saving his ammunition and not taking part in the fight. Of Tulley's and Bergstrom's fate he had no idea, but they were still inside the house. Slocum looked around and saw the men coming up the hillside. There were dozens of them, far more than he had thought. There was no way of escaping the cordon.

"Fight fire with fire," Slocum said to himself. He looked around and found enough straw to put together in a bundle. Affixing it to the end of a pitchfork, he lit it. The flambeau blazed in the darkness. He applied it to various spots around the barn, then walked calmly in the middle of the flying bullets and dropped the torch through the house's broken window.

Seconds later, both Tulley and Bergstrom came running from inside. The confusion of shooting at Tulley, trying not to kill their boss, and of figuring out what was happening, caused confusion to reign supreme in the guards' ranks.

Slocum could have escaped in the chaos, but he held back when he saw the expression on Bergstrom's face. There was fear, but there was something more. Fear for himself was mixed with fear of losing all he had stolen.

The banker made a beeline for his hidden loot. And John Slocum followed.

20

Slocum stood quietly and watched the conflagration. There was something compelling about the way the long tongues of bright orange flame devoured Bergstrom's house. Demons from hell couldn't have done a better job than the one Slocum had done. More important to him, the banker had hightailed it out, and he didn't look as if he was just running for his life.

The expression on his face told Slocum the man feared for the safety of the stolen money. It hadn't been hidden in the house. If it had, Bergstrom would have been screaming to the army of guards to put out the fire. As it was, he ignored them and the fire and just ran.

Slocum trailed him at a safe distance, keeping an eye out for Tulley. He had lost sight of the bounty hunter in the confusion. Both he and the banker had exploded from the house after Slocum torched it, but the bounty hunter had vanished in the bedlam.

"Fire!" someone yelled, as if it wasn't immediately obvious. "Get water. Put it out, or the whole dang prairie will catch fire. We'll never stop it, if it gets off the hillside!"

Slocum did nothing to help form a bucket brigade from the well just down the hill. Instead, he followed the banker, then stopped and stared.

"Now if that don't beat all," said to himself. Marcus Bergstrom had left his burning house and had made straight for the outhouse. Not even a man with the trots needed an outhouse when his home was burning down around his ears. That is, he didn't head for the little house unless there was something a sight more important in it than a wood seat, a few corncobs, and a deep hole.

Slocum forgot Tulley and the fire and the guards trying vainly to put out the fire. He homed in on the banker and his curious quest for the outhouse. It took only a few seconds to figure out the banker wasn't sitting inside thinking about the whichness of the why.

"Slocum," came a deep-throated roar. "I want you. I want you so bad I can taste it!"

Slocum swung around, his six-shooter coming up. The pistol's steel barrel crashed into the side of the bounty hunter's head, stunning him. The huge brute of a man sank down, but his arms flailed about. He caught Slocum behind the left knee with a hard punch and brought him down. More unconscious than aware of what he was doing, Tulley fought and got on top of the smaller Slocum.

Slocum grunted and heaved, arching his back. He threw Tulley off, but the mountain of gristle and bone crouched, ready to lunge again. The only good thing about the situation that Slocum could see was that Tulley had lost his monstrous shotgun.

"I don't want to plug you," Slocum said, aiming his pistol squarely at the bounty hunter.

"Why not? You done everything you could to kill me up till now," Tulley growled. He lumbered forward.

"You were trying to take me in. That poster's no good. It was all a mistake," Slocum lied. He tried to remember if he had fired his pistol after reloading. The chaos surrounding the assault on Bergstrom's house had distracted him. He might have all six rounds left; he might have only one or two.

One or two slugs from the Colt Navy weren't enough to stop the bounty hunter.

"What're you sayin', Slocum?" Tulley stopped and glared at him, his giant fists opening and closing slowly, as if seeking a neck to break. "You got posters out on you all over the place."

"They were wrong. The man who did those robberies was caught and convicted." Slocum tried to sound convincing. He had slowed the giant's advance. Frantically, Slocum looked over Tulley's shoulder at the outhouse. Bergstrom was still working on the roof, using his fingers to pry a section off. The money had to be hidden there and Slocum was losing it by arguing with the bounty hunter.

All he had to do was pull the trigger. He had one round left. He knew that much. He might have more. One well-placed shot would end the man's life. But Slocum didn't fire. He didn't much care for Tulley or his idea of personal cleanliness, but he had come to admire the big oaf's skill in tracking and his determination.

To kill him would be a waste. To kill the thieving, sneaky Marcus Bergstrom would benefit everyone in Grandville.

"I wouldn't be saying this to you if I wasn't being framed," Slocum said.

"That little wart of a teller. He came to me and said you was here. Even if you're right about the other crimes, and I ain't sayin' you are, the ones you upped and destroyed the posters and arrest warrants for, the law wants you in Grandville. You robbed their damned bank and set fire to their town."

"I didn't do those crimes, either," Slocum said. "Berg-strom robbed his own bank because he'd been sucking off money from it for years. This covered his theft."

"What about settin' fire to the place to escape the jail? You can't lie your way out of that."

"I don't know who started the fire. My friend and I were lucky to escape with our lives. Hell, we even saved the depu-ties who were guarding us. Somebody must have mentioned that. Does that sound like we were desperate criminals?"

"A deputy did say something about that, but he also said you started the fire."

"They don't know what caused it," Slocum went on. He was getting impatient. He didn't want to fight Tulley, but he wasn't going to be able to convince him in time to stop Bergstrom, either. It took the bounty hunter too long to work things through in his head.

"Why'd that little teller say you'd done it, then?" Tulley looked perplexed at such heavy thinking.

"He's in it with the banker. They're in cahoots."

Tulley growled deep in his throat. Slocum saw the fire in the man's eyes and knew he hadn't convinced him. Horace Wainwright hadn't stayed scared long enough for Slocum's comfort. He had probably rushed out just after Slocum left his house, found the bounty hunter, and told him where Slocum was headed.

That also meant Wainwright would tell the sheriff event-ually. Not only Tulley and Bergstrom's army were here, the sheriff and his posse would be showing up sooner or later. If the fire didn't bring them, Wainwright would.

Slocum fired just past Tulley's head. The giant bounty hunter twitched as if a mosquito had nipped at his ear and kept coming. Slocum considered emptying his six-shooter into the man, however many rounds remained. It wouldn't be as if he killed him in cold blood. Tulley was more than a match for Slocum physically, outweighing him by at least a hundred pounds.

At the last possible instant, Slocum sidestepped and swung his pistol again. He caught the bounty hunter right behind the ear and sent him tumbling down the hillside. A whiff of smoke blew past and Slocum gagged on it. When the wind had cleared away the smoke, he looked for Tulley. The man had disappeared in a welter of horses and men at the base of the hill. Slocum thought the sheriff might have arrived, but he wasn't sure.

He didn't have any time left. He had wasted too much time with the bounty hunter. Checking his Colt Navy, he saw he had only a single round left. It would have to do; he didn't have the time or the ammunition to reload.

Marcus Bergstrom had finished prying off the lid of the small compartment he'd built into the roof of his outhouse. Slocum studied the situation and then smiled. The light from the fire gave him just enough illumination to see his target. His Colt Navy came up and fired. The bullet flew straight and true to its target.

Bergstrom let out a yelp that could have been heard ten miles away. He dropped the large, canvas-wrapped bundle he had wrestled from the hiding place and lit out running. He swatted at the hornets buzzing around his ears. Slocum's bullet had found its target in the center of a large nest hanging just inches away from Bergstrom's face. The angry hornets had taken out their ire at having their nest disturbed on the first victim they could find.

The banker ran down the hill. The dark cloud following him made it appear he was on fire. And he would be, if he didn't outrun the hornets soon.

Slocum swatted at a few of the angry insects as he hefted the package Bergstrom had dropped. He opened one corner and looked inside. A huge smile crossed his face. The bag was stuffed with greenbacks. He had finally recovered what he had set out to find.

"There! There he is, men. Get him!" came the sheriff's shout from near what was left of Bergstrom's house.

Slocum lit out after the banker, knowing he was the object of the sheriff's hunt. With the money in his possession now, he wasn't going to give up easily.

21

Slocum was under a severe handicap trying to hang onto the bundle of money and not be shot by the deputies firing at him from behind. He finally gave up trying to dodge the deputies so hot in pursuit and just concentrated on keeping his feet moving straight ahead. If he ran fast enough, he'd outrun them and could get to his horse. They'd ridden hard from Grandville to help with the fire. His horse had been resting for a couple of hours while he scouted the Bergstrom house. If he could outdistance them, he'd soon be free and rich.

His feet got tangled up in some undergrowth and Slocum fell head over heels down the hillside. This did more to put distance between him and the lawmen than his own efforts had. He fetched up hard against a rock, still clutching the canvas bundle to his chest. He heard pistols firing and felt sharp jerks. For a second he was too stunned to know what was happening. Then he realized that the deputies were firing at him and their bullets were being absorbed by the money bag.

Slocum swung around, aimed, and fired. The bullet winged a deputy and sent the others scurrying for cover.

The Colt's hammer rose and fell again, this time hitting an empty chamber. He was out of ammunition without time to reload. Slocum had to use the brief seconds before the posse got their courage screwed up enough to attack again to get the hell away.

He almost went limp with relief when he saw his roan standing and contentedly munching at dried grass. Slocum had precious little time to securely fasten the money to the rear of his saddle. He lashed it down the best he could, using the leather thongs on his saddle skirt. Vaulting into the saddle, he stayed low and urged his horse away.

More lead flew around him. He thought he might have to drag out his trusty Winchester and return fire, but the sheriff's voice echoed down the hill.

"Let him go. We'll get him later. We got to put the fire out now. It's spreadin' something fierce."

The deputies broke off the fight and returned to help extinguish the blaze. Slocum felt no sense of achievement at almost causing such a major disaster. If the fire found a foothold on the prairie, everyone in Grandville would be burned out.

He didn't feel good about that, but everything else caused him to glow inside. He had the money from the robbery. He had finally gotten away from Tulley. And he had his revenge on Marcus Bergstrom. Taking the money was probably the sweetest retaliation he could have wreaked on the banker. Bergstrom had stolen the money and had lost it. That and the pain he would get from the hornets gave Slocum a sense of satisfaction that justice had been done.

Justice had been done and he had eighteen thousand dollars riding behind him.

Slocum rode hard, varying the pace so his roan wouldn't drop under him. By noon, he was twenty miles away from Grandville. Alternately walking and riding took him another five miles by sundown. Then he stepped up the pace again after finding water for his horse. Past midnight, Slocum paused to rest.

He shot and killed a rabbit and was roasting it as he leafed through the pile of greenbacks. Curious, Slocum began counting. When he was finished he frowned. He had only four thousand dollars, a princely sum, but nowhere near the full amount Bergstrom had claimed.

"I'll be hornswoggled," Slocum muttered to himself. He had told Tulley that the banker had been embezzling and had used the theft as a way of covering up past crimes. Slocum had made it up, but now he realized this was what had really happened. Bergstrom had been stealing steadily from his depositors. The robbery had given him the chance to make a few extra thousand dollars and hide what he had stolen over the years.

"Four thousand dollars," Slocum said. It wasn't as much as he'd thought, but it was enough—more than enough—to pay him back for his backbreaking efforts digging in the mines, being locked up, and being chased to hell and gone by the bounty hunter.

Slocum's hand flashed to his pistol when he heard a sound behind him.

"Tulley!" he cried, thinking the bounty hunter had again tracked him down.

Then the stars spun in wild circles around his head. A rifle barrel had swung through the air and connected with the top of his head. He tried to squeeze off a shot. His Colt Navy was pulled from his numb fingers. He tried to focus his eyes and couldn't do it. But he knew someone was taking the money.

"Tulley! I'll kill you for this. I will!" he promised.

Rage burned in his arteries. Slocum jerked around and his fingers closed on a boot. He jerked hard and almost upended the man stealing the money.

"Don't do it, John. I do declare, I don't want to shoot you for the money, but I will."

The voice brought him fully back to consciousness.

"Emmett!"

Slocum stared down a rifle barrel.

"I do hate to do this to you, John. We are friends, but I need the money. I saw you counting it. If there'd been the eighteen thousand we thought, I'd be happy to share. But I can't. I got big debts back in KC. This will only just cover them."

"Emmett, why are you doing this?"

"John, old son, I like you and consider you a friend, but I need the money bad."

Slocum glared at Emmett Vinson. "Did you ever think you could have just asked me for the money?"

Vinson looked startled, then a slow smile crossed his lips. "Never thought on it much. I just caught sight of you riding like a demon and followed. Took me all this time to catch up. I hadn't even planned to snoop on you the way I did."

"You could have taken the money, Emmett. This isn't going to sit well with me now, though."

"I don't want to kill you, John. I like you. I respect you. If there'd been more, well—" Vinson shrugged. "Too bad there wasn't more for our efforts."

"Are you going to gun me down in cold blood?"

Vinson shook his head sadly. "I'm sorry you could ever think that, John. If I'd got away with the money and you hadn't known who robbed you, that would have been for the best. Now there's going to be a festering between us. don't much like that, but I can't bring myself to kill you."

"So what's it going to be?" Slocum looked around for some way of keeping the money. In spite of Vinson' backstabbing actions, he wasn't up to gunning the ma down, either. Vinson might not be a friend any longer, but Slocum didn't cotton much to shooting him.

He didn't cotton much to losing the money, either.

"I'll tie you up. You can get free before any of the posse after you can arrive."

"You've seen someone on my trail?"

"Nary a soul," Vinson said, "but there's got to be someone after you. You've got the money from the Grandville bank. I'm real curious about the details on where you found it, but there're more important things on my mind than a good yarn."

Slocum heard movement behind Vinson and saw a large shadow appear. He started to speak, then clamped his mouth shut. He gauged the distance to his bedroll and the Winchester hidden there. Vinson had taken his Colt. Slocum needed a rifle to stop the bounty hunter.

"You started to warn me about someone behind me, didn't you, John? Thank you for not trying that hoary old chestnut. It's so old a trick that it's got moss growing on—"

The tree limb whished through the air and connected squarely with the side of Vinson's head. The man's legs buckled, and he fell bonelessly, like a marionette with its strings cut.

Slocum was already in motion, diving level with the ground and landing hard. He kicked twice and covered the remaining distance between him and his rifle.

"Don't," came the soft command.

Slocum looked up and saw Marla Vinson standing over her brother. She held the tree branch in her hands. She dropped it and brushed her hands off on her dress.

"He always was too greedy for his own good," she said. "Are you all right, John?"

Slocum didn't see any weapon. She had used the tree branch but not a rifle or the heavy six-shooter she was so expert with. He could still get to his Winchester and—and what? He was too confused to know what was happening.

"I'm a tad befuddled over this turn of affairs," Slocum said. He didn't pull his rifle out of its scabbard. He wanted to hear what Marla had to say.

"Emmett got involved with a gang of gamblers in Kansas City. If he ever wanted to go back there, he had to pay off his gambling losses."

"Why bother going back? The West is big enough to—"

He stopped when Marla shook her head. She looked like an angel in the faint light cast by his campfire. In spite of everything that had happened, he found himself wanting her.

"Emmett doesn't have good sense when it comes to women. He's sweet on a gambler's daughter. He knows he'd never see her again if he didn't pay his debts."

"If she likes him, she could run away with him," suggested Slocum.

"That's a logical conclusion to something that has no logic," Marla said. She lifted Slocum's pistol from her brother's gun belt, then pulled his side arm from its holster. She picked up Emmett's rifle and stood by the fire, armed to the teeth.

Slocum tensed, waiting for what might happen. Marla walked around the fire, both six-shooters in her hands and the rifle under her arm.

"She's scared to death of her father and would never go against his wishes. Emmett thinks she'll come away with him if he gets her father's permission—by paying off his gambling losses."

"That's crazy," Slocum said.

"That's Emmett." Marla said it as if all things were explained. "He really does like you. I hope you won't hold this lapse against him. He's torn between what he thinks is true love and your friendship."

"That's a good way to get killed."

Marla laughed. "That's true, John, that's so very true." She held up the six-shooters, then tossed Slocum's ebony-handled Colt to him. He caught it, his index finger sliding through the trigger guard and his thumb bringing back the hammer.

He aimed the pistol squarely at her. She made no move to raise her brother's pistol.

"Why'd you slug him?"

"I don't even like that bitch back in KC," Marla said. "Why should I let him louse up his life by stealing the money from you?"

"And?" Slocum prodded. There was more. There had to be more.

"There's no logic to true love. I'd cross even my own brother for you, John Slocum."

He lowered the hammer on the Colt and slid the weapon back into his cross-draw holster.

"There's more to it than that, isn't there, Marla."

"There's always more, John," she said with a laugh. "Keeping Emmett from the money prevents him from making a fool of himself and wasting four thousand dollars. And it wasn't right for him to take the money from you like he was planning."

She came over and gently stroked his cheek. "I do love you, John, but I also want my share of the money."

It was Slocum's turn to laugh. "How do we divvy it up?"

"You have four thousand. You could keep all of it, and you'd have both Emmett and me on your trail to get our share."

"Or we could divide it in half. Two thousand dollars is powerful lot of money," Slocum said.

"We could do it that way," Marla agreed. He saw a little sadness in her at the suggestion.

"Or there's another way," Slocum said. He started counting out the money into three equal piles. "Emmett gets his share." Slocum took the other two piles and put it back into his saddlebags.

"And?" Marla asked, intrigued by what he was doing.

"And you and me ride on out right now and spend the rest of it together. Maybe Denver, maybe San Francisco."

"But not Kansas City," Marla said.

Slocum found himself with an armful of woman intent on kissing him. That, and the money, suited him just fine.